Wolf Pack

Bridget Essex

Wolf Pack

Other Books by Bridget Essex

Meeting Eternity (The Sullivan Vampires, Vol. 1)
Trusting Eternity (The Sullivan Vampires, Vol 2)
The Protector
Wolf Heart
Wolf Queen
Falling for Summer
The Guardian Angel
The Vampire Next Door (with Natalie Vivien)
A Wolf for Valentine's Day
A Wolf for the Holidays
The Christmas Wolf
Don't Say Goodbye
Forever and a Knight
A Knight to Remember
Date Knight
Wolf Town
Dark Angel
Big, Bad Wolf

Erotica

Wild
Come Home, I Need You

Wolf Pack

About the Author

My name is Bridget Essex, and I've been writing about vampires for almost two decades. I'm influenced most by classic vampires— the vision of CARMILLA (it's one of the oldest lesbian novels!) and DRACULA. My vampires have always been kind of traditional (powerful), but with the added self-torture of regret and the human touch of guilt.

I have a vast collection of knitting needles and teacups, and like to listen to classical music when I write. My first date with my wife was strolling in a garden, so it's safe to say I'm a bit old fashioned. I have a black cat I love very much, and two white dogs who actually convince me to go outside. When I'm actually outside, I begin to realize that writing isn't all there is to life. Just most of it! I'm married to the love of my life, author Natalie Vivien.

Find out more about my work at
www.LesbianRomance.org and
http://BridgetEssex.Wordpress.com

Wolf Pack
Copyright © 2016 Bridget Essex - All Rights Reserved
Published by Rose and Star Press
First edition, April 2016

This is a work of fiction. Names, characters, places and incidents either are products of the author's imagination or are used fictitiously. Any resemblance to actual events or locales or persons, living or dead, is entirely coincidental.

This book, or parts thereof, may not be reproduced without written permission.

ISBN: 1532808887
ISBN-13: 978-1532808883

Wolf Pack

Wolf Pack

DEDICATION

For Natalie, always.

Wolf Pack

-- Wolf Heart --

"Honey, I'm not trying to dissuade you or anything, but it's common knowledge that people who go camping alone in national parks around Halloween almost always end up murdered."

I burst out laughing as I put on my turn signal. My cell phone headset crackles with static as I pull off the main highway, route 86, and head deeper into the mountains of Allegany State Park.

"But what you're saying right now is that my camping alone is *definitely* going to lead to my murder. I think that counts as dissuading, Mom," I tell her with a shake of my head, chuckling into my Bluetooth headset. "Thanks for the confidence, by the way," I smirk. "Didn't *you* camp at the family campsite *alone* when you were *sixteen?*"

"That was a different time," my mother tells me dismissively, and I can almost see her brandishing her coffee mug as she launches into, "There were *far* fewer serial killers when I was a young woman."

I laugh again as I turn on my brights. The moment I coast beneath the brooding pine trees surrounding the entrance to the state park, the darkness eats up my headlights, and putting on my brights does very little to help with the visibility. I roll down my windows to smell the autumn leaves and the bracing, chill October air; it makes me shiver. Everything here is muffled and dark, which probably sounds much creepier than it actually is...

Okay. I'm lying. It's actually pretty creepy right now. I've never arrived at the park so late in the day, or you know, *night,* and I didn't expect it to be this pitch black. And, to add to the creepy ambiance, I'm driving down a deserted, dark road in the middle of nowhere the day before Halloween. This moment is pretty much a reenactment of the opening of every Halloween movie I've ever seen...

Even as I have that thought, a deer darts out right in front of me, bounding out of the thick forest of pine trees to the left, long legs flexing as she hurtles across the pavement, scrambling with her dainty hooves for purchase on the road, skidding on it since she's running so quickly. She is *right* in front of the nose of my car, and there's probably not enough time to avoid hitting her, but all I am in that moment is one giant reflex.

I gasp as I slam on the brakes.

Thankfully, I was already reducing my speed; the speed limit is thirty-five miles-per-hour through Allegany, and I already got a ticket here once—issued by an unhappy park ranger/security guy. And I'll be damned if I'm getting a ticket again! So when I slam on the brakes, the car slows down quickly, and nothing terrible happens. I'm able to stop my car just shy of the doe, who actually came to a halt in front of my fender, staring at it with wide, unblinking eyes. Apparently, deer aren't the smartest of creatures.

I pant, gripping the steering wheel tightly as we stare at each other, the doe and me. Her wide, wet eyes are framed by long, delicate lashes, and I'm so close that I can see her small nose wrinkling in distress as she huffs a breath that curls out into the air like smoke. Breathless, I watch this gorgeous creature—this gorgeous creature that I almost just turned into roadkill. I swallow, trying to quell my adrenaline, and then the spell is broken: the doe darts off again, taking a single, powerful bound to clear the rest of the road and disappear on the other side, into the thicket. And, that fast, in a single heartbeat, she's gone.

"Abby? Abby, honey, are you okay?" comes my mom's panicked voice from my headset. Crap—with all the adrenaline pouring through me, I completely forgot I was on the phone. My mom says, all in a rush, "I just heard the brakes screeching!"

"I'm okay, Mom," I tell her, forcing out a laugh that sounds fake even to me, the one faking it. I gulp down air and take another deep breath, letting it out slowly. Then I adjust the earpiece. "Sorry. A deer just jumped out in front of me, but I didn't hit her. I just had to brake hard. I'm fine, car's fine, deer's fine. It's all good." I grip the steering wheel, my knuckles white in the dark.

"See, that's one of the million reasons you shouldn't be doing this," my mom frets. "If you wanted to play at Annie Oakley, you could come camp in our backyard! Heaven knows it's a jungle out there," she tells me with a long sigh.

I'm laughing again, and my body begins to relax as I put my foot on the gas, crawling into the park now. I'm going so slow that my speedometer doesn't even flick over the number "5" for a few minutes.

"I'd hardly call your tiny backyard in south Buffalo a jungle, Mom," I tease her gently, smiling as I grip the steering wheel a little less tightly now. I roll my shoulders back. "Just remind Dad that I'll be visiting you guys after the camping trip. I'll be breaking camp on Monday morning, so I'll drive into town and expect Tim Hortons coffee and donuts pretty much right away."

My mom is chuckling, but I can still hear the worry in her voice. "Just don't eat a half dozen Boston creams in one sitting like last time, okay?"

"I'm offended," I smile. "You know Jack helped me." Jack is my parents' very, very elderly Boston Terrier, and by "helping me," I mean that he might have licked a drop of custard off of my finger, if I remember correctly.

"Abby..." my mother starts, and I know she's about to launch into one last-ditch effort to keep me from camping alone this weekend.

So I beat her to it.

"Look, I just really needed to get away," I tell her, my voice calm, soothing, the exact voice I use when my dog, Peanut, sits quaking under the bed during thunderstorms and I have to coax her out. "I'll be safe," I say, smiling, reassuring, calm. "I mean, I'm staying in our cabin; it's got two locks! An impenetrable fortress with two locks. And I'm sure there are other people camping, because seasoned campers know that the week before Halloween is less crowded. And there are park rangers all over the place... Besides all of that, the park just isn't full of serial killers, no matter what you say, Mom," I tell her with a sigh. "Deer, yeah. There are a lot of deer," I concede with a chuckle. "But I don't think murder is on their agenda. Unless they try to run into my car again."

"Well," says my mother, sounding very unsure. "I know you're going to do what you want to do,

Abby," she finally tells me, with a very long-suffering sigh. "And I know you can take care of yourself."

"I didn't take all those karate lessons when I was a kid for nothing!"

"Just promise me you'll be careful?" she says, with another very long sigh.

"I promise," I tell her soothingly. And then, very quickly, I belt out, "I love you and Dad. I'll see you very soon! And I'm going up the mountain, so I'm losing the signal. I'll have to let you go! I love you! Bye!" I tell her all in a single breath, and before she can tack on another, "I'm not sure this trip is a good idea" speech to the three *dozen* that she already gave me on the car ride here, I cut the connection, tossing my Bluetooth onto the seat next to me.

I take a deep breath and roll my shoulders back again; I'm stiff from the long drive—and from being so tense throughout the conversation. I mean, I knew my mother wouldn't be happy that I was taking a camping trip alone. Camping alone is Not Done so late in the season, according to her. But I also know that I'm perfectly safe here. After all, I've been coming to Allegany State Park since I was a baby—literally. My parents brought me to the cabin for the very first time when I was thirty days old. And, completely TMI, but when my mother was drunk at my uncle's New Year's party once, she told me that I was conceived in that very same cabin, so you could kind of say that camping is in my blood. I've been here so many times that I know this place like the back of my hand. Yeah, there are bears here, but they're small black bears who crave wild-grown blackberries and campers' trash, rather than, well, the campers themselves. There is nothing dangerous in this entire park except for bad compasses and a bad sense of direction: a few folks died here while hiking, after getting lost.

But other than that...I'm perfectly safe.

And, hell, I've gone two years without taking time off from work. I've won so many attendance gold stars at this point (I work in telemarketing, and they love handing out gold stars to the drudges who manage to show up every day), I could fill a jar with them.

I *need* this vacation.

I could never tell you exactly why I put off taking a vacation during the nice, summer months, the months when the cabin was completely empty, when I could have gone swimming in the pond, eaten ice cream and popsicles from the General Store and sunned myself on the little spit of beach. Maybe it's because I wanted time alone, time to myself, not to have to fight the crowd for the best spots. Autumn's my favorite season, so that factored into it, too. Autumn in Allegany State Park, straddling the border of New York and Pennsylvania, is breathtaking. The trees are a riot of colors, a treasure trove of autumn-hued gems, and even though it's dark out, I can smell autumn in the air. I can't wait to wake up tomorrow morning and look out my window at the beauty that surrounds me.

I guess I feel silly saying that I felt called to come to the park this week, but that's the absolute truth of it. I had a dream one night, a dream of me walking through the woods in the twilight hours, beneath the amber-colored trees, feeling perfectly happy and content. I woke up, and I still felt that happiness and contentment, at least for a little while. It lasted in me like a memory, even though I hadn't experienced it. And that sealed the deal. I *wanted* that. And now, here

I am.

Much to my mother's dismay.

I roll through the Quaker section of the park. Allegany State Park is divided into two distinct areas, with a mountain in between. One side is called Red House; that's where the "rich" people go to camp. Well, they aren't necessarily rich, but that's what it seemed like to me when I was a kid. And then there's the Quaker side, what my mother calls "the plebeian side" of the mountain.

I turn my car into the small gravel parking lot for the rental station.

Our family has owned a cabin on the Quaker side for at least two generations. The cabin was here before they offered camping at the park, so we were sort of grandfathered into the whole park system. I don't need a key to get into our family cabin—I have one—but it's just common courtesy to tell the rangers that I'm here and give them some sort of time frame for how long I think I'll stay.

I turn off the engine and my headlights. Immediately, I'm plunged into thick darkness. Gingerly, I open the car door, and as the cold air gusts into my car, I'm surprised—as I always am at this time of year—that there's not a single sound in the forest surrounding me. All of the bugs are dead or sleeping for the winter, and the smaller forest animals have gone to bed for the night. The birds have either flown away or are nestled asleep somewhere. So, right now, the woods are still, so quiet that I can hear myself breathing. I can even hear my heartbeat in my chest, the steady *thump-thump, thump-thump* speeding up a little, just because the woods, at night, would make anyone's heart beat a little faster.

It's a disconcerting feeling—especially for someone used to the hustle and bustle of Rochester—as I shut my car door, and the sound of it echoes away into the darkness, muffled into silence by the close, brooding pine trees. I burrow my hands deep into my jacket pockets, turning up my fleece's collar to stave off the chill that's rolling in off the pond, and I trot up the three steps to the station's front door. I'm glad to see that there's a small light on inside, the tiny warmth of it spilling out onto the wooden boards of the porch. But when I peer through the window into the station itself, my heart sinks.

I was kind of hoping that Bob or Sherri or Alex would be on duty tonight. I've been camping here for so long that I know every ranger, and most of them I love.

Except for one.

The one in the station right now.

Barbara.

Barbara has been a park ranger here at Allegany since I was a kid, and she knows my family and me pretty well. And because of that, and because I love the park so much, I kind of feel like it's my duty to say all the usual, nice things about her, like Barbara is perfectly...well, *nice,* and she's always treated my family well, going so far as to track down my childhood dog, Socks, when she slipped out of the cabin one night when I was thirteen. I mean, that's *nice*. She didn't have to do that for us.

But even when I was little, there was something about her that made me uneasy. Maybe it's the way that she would look at us kids disapprovingly, like we were always up to something bad, even though we weren't. Maybe it's how she dragged my dog back when she found him, his tail between his legs as she gripped his collar so hard that there were brush-burn marks on his neck when she handed him over to us.

Barbara is also majorly into hunting, and as a vegetarian, hunting isn't really my favorite topic. But it was more than opposing views on things, more than the way my dog collapsed into my arms when Barbara returned him, as if she'd terrified him completely.

It's just that, sometimes, when Barbara looks at me—okay, I know this sounds weird. But it almost looks like she's staring at something, well...delicious. Like she's hungry, and I might be the sort of snack that's perfectly acceptable to devour before dinner.

Granted, these are the stories that kids tell each other when they're staying up past their bedtime, using flashlights like props, beams aimed under their chins while they mutter in spooky voices about the scariest scenarios they can come up with. And I did exactly that with my cousins when we'd camp here each summer. We would always try to outdo ourselves, coming up with the creepiest tales we could imagine...

And when we'd bring up Barbara (because of *course* we'd bring up Barbara), we'd talk in hushed tones about how she ate kids and stray pets. That last part was added onto the story after she brought our dog back. We said that she was part beast, because her teeth were a little sharper than everyone else's. Which wasn't actually true, but that's how it felt to me. There was something almost animal-like about Barbara.

Something that felt...amiss.

Even now, thinking about those childhood stories we'd tell each other...it makes me shiver as I glance in the window, as I see Barbara sitting at the ranger's desk, typing something up on the monolithic desktop computer, her eyes narrowed as she frowns at the screen.

There's something off-putting about her. Something that makes my mouth go dry.

Okay, okay, I know that's crazy. And I'm blaming all of my mother's talk about serial killers and cannibals for my reticence to raise my hand and knock on that ranger station door. Barbara is just...*intense* is all. And she doesn't have that many social skills, which is why her intensity always comes off as something uncomfortable. It's *not her fault*. But as I do fist my hand, poised to knock, I have to take a deep breath to still my thundering heartbeat.

C'mon, Abby, I cajole myself. *What's the worst she's going to do? She's not going to* bite *you.*

But, still, it takes me a moment to summon the courage to knock on that door.

The *knock, knock, knock* of my knuckles against the heavy wood sounds extra loud in the stillness of the night. I take a step back from the door, and I can hear someone with heavy boots moving across the floor inside. *Thump, thump.* I turn up my fleece collar even more, shivering in the cold air, and then I take a deep breath as the door opens in front of me, the soft light inside the ranger station spilling out onto the front porch.

"Abby Reynolds," says Barbara, her voice low, her tone disapproving. She has the advantage of the light being behind her, and of my eyes being adjusted to absolute blackness. So when she speaks to me, I really can't see her face; it's shrouded in darkness. But it doesn't take sight to understand that she's pretty unhappy to see me; her tone clearly conveyed that. She practically spat out my name.

"Well. Come on in," she grunts; then she's standing aside, and I walk into the station, the coolness of the air outside cut off as she shuts the door behind me and the warmth of the room washes over me.

Barbara stands about a head taller than me, even though I'm pretty tall myself. She has the kind of muscular build that suggests she works out all the time, and that's impressive. Honestly, it seems as if she hasn't changed much at all since the last time I've seen her.

It's kind of alarming, actually. Like she just doesn't age.

And when my gaze finally adjusts to the light and I can actually look her in the eyes, I'm doubly alarmed to see something that she never had before: a bright white scar passing over her right eye and onto her cheek. It's a thin, narrow slash that looks like it was probably pretty painful to endure.

Now she's staring at me with anger, glaring. Her lips move up over her teeth in a *snarl* as she gazes at me in bare disgust.

I take a step back, feeling chilled, wary. Yeah, I'd say it's pretty obvious that she's more unhappy to see me than ever before.

I wish I knew what I'd done to make her hate me so much. The worst thing I ever did to her was be frightened of her. And I used that fright to fuel some pretty outrageous stories after dark, flashlight beam pointed at my chin.

"Hi, Barbara. How are you?" I ask her, clearing my throat as I force a small smile onto my face. I hold out my hand to her for a shake.

But she doesn't take it. Instead, she deliberately glances down at it, her lips curling up even further over her teeth. She actually laughs, then, a short, sharp bark of a laugh as she shakes her head, turning away from me.

Barbara frowns as she sits down behind the desk, steepling her fingers over her middle. Then she sighs and pushes her chair back, glancing back up at my face again. Her eyes are narrowed and flashing with something I can't quite place. Agitation? Annoyance?

She wastes no time, just gets right down to business. "I'm displeased that you chose to camp here this week, Ms. Reynolds," she says, her voice strained, forced. "I really wish there was something I could do to talk you out of staying tonight." When she says this, her head is tilted to the side, her eyes slitted as she pins me to the spot with her hard gaze. Her brunette hair—though she's at least sixty, there's not a single streak of gray in it—is pulled back severely from her face, highlighting the scar. And her scowl.

I watch Barbara in shock, opening and shutting my mouth.

Before I can even think, I'm stating the obvious. "I...I'm sorry. I don't know why my staying at the cabin would bother you," I tell her quickly, spreading my hands as I stare at her, perplexed. "My family's cabin doesn't really even have anything to do with the park," I tell her, my voice shaking, nervous. I could count on my mother being worried about me, but I wasn't expecting there to be resistance from someone who has nothing to do with me or my life. Someone I'm checking in with, out of courtesy. There's no rule that says we have to stop at the ranger station before we go to our cabin; we've just always done it.

"There's a dangerous animal on the loose here," she says, the words coming out low, slow.

Well. That was unexpected. I blink.

"Dangerous animal? A bear? But you guys have bears all the time," I tell her.

She's shaking her head slowly, still keeping me within her angry sights. "No—not a bear," she growls, her eyes glinting as she stares up at me from her chair. She licks her lips, takes a deep breath. "There have been reports," she says, "that what we're dealing with..." She draws out a long breath, still glowering.

"What?" I mutter.

She holds my gaze. "A wolf," she says simply.

And I laugh—until I realize that she's not laughing, too. And, anyway, she doesn't strike me as the type of person who cracks jokes.

Ever.

"How is that possible?" is what I finally settle on replying. When I was a little girl, I thought I heard wolves howling out in the woods, but it was never really wolves. Coyotes occasionally, yeah, but wolves haven't been wild here since well over a hundred years ago.

She shrugs, but she's still staring at me shrewdly, her eyes narrowed. "So, it's not safe for you to—"

"Reports?" I ask her, folding my arms in front of me. "What kind of reports? Have there been sightings of this wolf? Where could the wolf possibly have come from? A zoo? Wouldn't I have heard about it?"

She says nothing for a long moment, only stares at me, her eyes boring into my skull in an invasive fashion. Finally, she says, "I urge you—*strongly*—not to camp here at the park this weekend, Ms. Reynolds." Her voice is voice sharp, clipped, succinct. "But if you *want* to camp against my wishes, there is...*nothing* I can do to stop you."

Coupled with her sarcastic tone, her darkened eyes, and her scowling face, her words take on an ominous tone.

I stare, holding my tongue. I'm not intimidated by her, and I'm certainly not intimidated by an unlikely story about a wolf terrorizing Allegany State Park. That's like saying there's a sea-monster swimming in the lake. Both of those things are impossible.

I know Barbara has never liked me, and she doesn't want me staying in the park. But my camping plans have nothing to do with her.

It's been a long drive to get here, and I was already exhausted when I got off of work this afternoon. So what comes out next isn't something I'm exactly proud of.

"You've never liked me, Barbara," I say. Somewhere, far away, my sensible side is horrified at how flushed my cheeks are, at the impassioned words that are pouring out of my mouth. But I can't stop them. "But I don't honestly care. I'm camping here this week, and if you think your half-assed story frightens me, you have another think coming."

And then, internally mortified—*oh-God-I-can't-believe-I-just-did-that*—I turn around and aim for the door.

"Ms. Reynolds," says Barbara, her voice low, her tone thick with warning.

I can't help it. I stop, and I turn on my heel to look back at her.

My heartbeat leaps up into my throat, because when I look back...

She's staring at me. Her eyes are wide and wild-looking, and the way that she's smiling... Well, she's showing more teeth than people usually show when they smile.

It's...genuinely frightening.

"Watch out for wolves," she tells me, still smiling that scary, much-too-big smile. I open the door, and then I'm stumbling down the porch steps as her laughter, her genuine *laughter*, chases after me, out into the night.

I fall into my car, shove the key in the ignition, and then I'm driving away from the ranger station and the creepy woman that I told stories about when I was a kid, trying to make them scarier than the stories my cousins told, all about how Barbara would eat you up if you got on her bad side.

A feat I successfully accomplished tonight.

And the way she looked at me?

Yeah. Maybe those childhood stories had a hint of truth to them, after all.

I take a deep breath, trying to quell my too-fast heartbeat as I move down the road, between the thick layers of trees. She's not a friendly person; she just wanted to spook me. Part of me wonders if she'd go so far as to pull a prank or two out in the woods, try to get me to leave, but there's no *actual* reason for her to dislike me. I know all of her coworkers, her supervisor... If she did something to get me to leave the cabin, I would report her.

But what the hell was that—that smile, that laugh? What just happened?

I shake my head, rub my face with my right hand, keeping the left hand tight on the wheel.

That was just...weird.

The minute I get to the cabin, I park the car

and stare up at the usually comforting building. Our cabin looks like a lot of the other cabins in Allegany, with its small front porch, sharp-looking roof and warm, wooden shingles. And it usually *is* very comforting to see, filling me with a sense of ease, of rightness with the world.

But when I get out of the car right now, closing the door behind me, I'm plunged into darkness again. Honestly, I used to love the dark here when I was a kid. When it was summer, I'd catch fireflies, and when it was fall, we'd gather around campfires and tell each other spooky stories and eat s'mores until we got sick. I have a lot of good memories about nighttime here at Allegany Stare Park, but right now, I don't want to be in the dark, and I don't want to be faced with opening up the cabin, fumbling around with next-to-no visibility as I light my lantern, as I try to make the place feel safe.

So I grab my overnight bag from the backseat, and I find my flashlight in the glove compartment, and I set off down the worn, familiar path between the pines, leading to the bathroom.

One of the best things about my family's cabin has always been its closeness to one of the camp bathroom buildings. There are only a handful of bathrooms scattered through the Quaker section of Allegany State Park, and we happen to be close to the best one. Most of the camp bathrooms have showers on one side of the concrete block building, and toilets and sinks on the other, and this bathroom is no exception. But this building is longer, has more showers and toilet stalls, which means it has more lighting and also means, in summer, that if you get up early enough and sprint, you won't have to wait in line for a shower. And you *might* be lucky enough to get some hot water out of the deal, too.

So I follow the path, my flashlight on, beam down so that I don't startle any of the small wildlife or critters who might be out on such a cold night (though I doubt there are any; it's just habit). I have my bag slung over my shoulder, my left hand tucked deeply into my fleece pocket, as I mull over Barbara's ridiculous behavior and my own reaction to her. I'm embarrassed by how I responded, but I'm also upset by how *she* responded. And how very, very creepy she'd become within a manner of seconds.

Honestly, I hate to keep using the word "creepy." I usually only use that word for horror movies and poorly lit basements and horror movies *set* in poorly lit basements. But Barbara was the personification of all those things tonight.

So much for a relaxing start to the weekend!

But by the time I reach the bathroom building, I've convinced myself that I must have said or done something when I was a little kid to make her hate me, which means that, at least, she wasn't doing all of this stuff unprovoked. And, for some reason, that makes me feel better. I mean, I wasn't a *bad* kid, but I was by no saint, either. I got into trouble just as fast as—or perhaps a little faster than—my boy cousins when we went camping every year. I was a tomboy, and I often led the adventures into the mountains, my five cousins following behind me like my band of merry men. I was their sunburned, five-year-old girl version of Robin Hood.

Yes. When I was in the middle of one of my Robin Hood plays, I must have done something that rubbed Barbara in a very wrong way.

There. Now that I've convinced myself (not

Wolf Pack

really) of that fact, I can stop worrying about it.

And I sort of do stop worrying. I open the heavy metal door of the bathroom building and am immediately comforted by the bright fluorescent glow of the lights overhead. I close the door behind me, and for a long moment, I stand with my back to the door, my hand hovering over the lock. I consider locking the door behind me.

I grimace for a long moment, debating. If I lock the door, that would mean that I could take a shower in absolute peace, knowing that not a single soul would disturb me. But at the same time, I know that there *are* other campers at the park tonight (I saw a van down in one of the cabin rings)—and what if some poor drunk teenage girl needs to take a shower *really* badly? I can't deny anyone that. So, even though it's against my better judgment, I obey the wordless camping rules that I was raised on. Never deny a fellow camper a bathroom. It's just good karma.

I set my pack on the bench along the wall opposite the showers and rummage around in it for my bottles of shampoo, body wash and shaving cream, and my little painfully pink disposable razor. I'm purposefully thinking of a bunch of things *other* than Barbara right now, like wondering if I should go on another date with Stacey.

Yeah, Stacey. I'll think about Stacey.

I gather the bottles in my arms and deposit them in one of the empty shower stalls, as I ponder my not-girlfriend. Stacey is really nice; we went on a handful of dates this month, while also going on dates with other people. She's very pretty, with short red hair and big green eyes and this really cute nose. I liked her on sight. But Stacey just got out of a long-term relationship with a woman she was engaged to...and she said on the very first date that we should date other people while we also date each other. She made it painfully clear that we wouldn't be exclusive.

I turn on the hot water and hold my hand under the stream; it's shockingly cold, so I wait. I wait, and I wait, and finally, the hot water reaches me—and it's scalding. One moment, frozen water is pummeling the palm of my hand, and the next, it's water hot enough to boil a lobster. I wince and dial back the ancient water knobs a little; then I take a step back from the shower and unzip my fleece jacket.

Even though the steam from the shower is pouring into the room, I'm still shivering when I tug the jacket off over my shoulders, folding it into a pile on the bench. I'm just wearing a tank top beneath, and that comes off over my head in a second. I wad it up and toss it beside my fleece, running my hands through my hair as I take my ponytail holder out and toss it into my bag. I shake out my hair and groan a little as I flex backward, still stupidly sore from the drive here.

Yeah. Maybe I shouldn't think about Stacey. I don't know if that's a dead end, or if it's something that could possibly evolve into a relationship... It's just too uncertain. And I'm kind of sick of the uncertainties of life.

I peel my jeans over my legs and take them off, along with my panties. Then I remove my socks, too, after toeing off my hiking boots. I stand there naked for a moment, rubbing my shoulders and playing with the water's heat, fiddling with the knobs until it's the perfect temperature—and then I step under that blast of water.

I gasp, letting the heat sluice over me, chasing

away all of the cold in an instant as I shiver in delight. I rub my hands over my eyes, my long, blonde hair running with water down my back, and for the first time all day, as I tilt my head back, letting the water rush over me, I exhale, relaxing.

I draw in long, slow breaths as the water pours over me, letting every bit of the tension in my shoulders pour out, too, as they relax, ease down. I lift up my arms, running my fingers through my hair, working out the tangles.

I'm so relaxed, in fact, with the water rushing around me so fast and hard, hammering my back and my head, that I almost don't hear the sound over the roar of the water...

But I do hear it.

My eyes go wide, and I gasp, grabbing the water knobs for a moment, gasping out water that I got in my nose as I try to hold my breath, try to listen.

And there it is again.

The first time, the sound that rose over the shower was this: the unmistakable creaking of the metal door opening.

And now it's the same creak, but in reverse. The door is shutting.

The door to the outside opened and shut.

Every hair on my body is at attention, and I'm covered in goosebumps as I grip the faucet knobs with knuckles so tight, they're white. I blink back the water running into my eyes, and I try to quell my panicked heartbeat. It's not unusual for someone else to come into the showers, obviously; there are other campers here this weekend.

But it's late. And that run-in with Barbara was so damn weird. I'm still on edge. I kept the bathroom door unlocked in case anyone else wanted to use it, but I honestly didn't think anyone *would* use it. I know that's not logical, but hearing the door open and shut unnerved me.

Normally, you acknowledge a fellow camper in the bathrooms only if you're both fully clothed, and even then, it's just a nod. You don't ever call out from your shower stall or yell "Hello!" at them.

And you certainly don't peer out at them from around the shower curtain like a weird person. But that's exactly what I'm thinking about doing right now.

I take a step forward on the slick concrete floor, my hand reaching out toward the drab, gray shower curtain as my heart beats uncontrollably inside of me.

I just... I just have to see who's out there. It'll just be a tiny peek. She probably won't even *see* me peeking.

I just have to know I'm safe. Barbara *did* get to me, as much as it pains me to admit it.

So I pull the shower curtain back a little, and I peer out of the tiny gap, toward the door.

The moment seems to crystallize around me. The water seems to slow; the rush spilling down all around me is muffled white noise as I listen to my ragged breathing. I stare from behind the shower curtain, the curtain that is now trembling because my hand is trembling. What I'm seeing out there, in the shower hall, makes my knees actually buckle, weakening. But I don't let them give out. I stiffen my legs, gaping.

What I'm seeing is... Well, I can't believe it's possible.

There's a wolf standing in the middle of the bathroom floor.

And it's bleeding.

The wolf is about as tall as my hips, big and lanky, with very dark brown fur that's mottled in places with black. It's wheezing, its nose wrinkling as it pants, bracing itself into a standing position on the concrete, its massive paws spread around it, quivering, trying to hold it up. Its claws are pressing, scraping against the concrete floor, and its right shoulder is actually dripping blood. There's a small pool of the red stuff gathered around its front right paw on the ground, spilling outward over the dirty concrete.

Gasping for air, I let the shower curtain fall back into place, and I stand there, under the powerful stream of water, and I don't know what to do. I *don't know what to do*.

There's a wolf in the bathroom.

A *wolf*.

I'm shaking, I realize, as I stare down at my wet hands, water dripping from the ends of my fingers as the shower goes on, as if nothing out of the ordinary is happening at all. I curl my hands tightly into fists, trying to think of something to do, anything I can do to get out of this. Adrenaline courses through me.

For a second, I wonder if I really saw what I *think* I saw. No, there is no way I could have. Right? I take a deep breath, letting it blow out my nose. My mind is desperately grappling, trying to substitute something else over the image of the wolf. Something else that actually makes *sense*.

It was a very long drive. I'm hyped up on caffeine. I'm really hungry. Don't people see things when they're starving? Yeah. That must be it. It *must* be.

But still, I take another step forward , and I'm

curling my fingers around the shower curtain again, bracing myself. I think about what Barbara said, about there being a wolf in the park. But a *wolf* in a state park in *New York*? It sounded crazy, unbelievable, when she told me that, with her narrowed gaze and that ridiculous smirk.

But I have to believe my own eyes, don't I?

I steel my nerves. I take a deep breath, and I hold it, and I pull the curtain back. I need to see if the wolf is real. If I made it up.

I must have made it up.

Because there isn't a wolf in the middle of the bathroom.

I stare at what *is* lying on the concrete floor, though, and everything seems to speed up around me again, the air pouring out of me as I gasp, as I fumble with the knobs on the shower, my entire body quaking as I manage to turn the water off and race out of the shower, naked and not even caring.

Because in the center of the bathroom floor, curled up into a tight ball, there is no wolf but a woman, just as naked as me.

And she's bleeding. Badly.

I almost slip on the concrete floor when I approach her, but I manage to catch myself from a complete fall, racing to a crouch beside the prone figure. I stare down, unsure of what to do as she curls up into a tighter ball, gasping herself.

She has her face pressed into her knees, her arms wrapped tightly around her legs, her body curled inward, but I can still make out some significant details. Like the fact that her right shoulder, the one that's facing the ceiling of the bathroom, since she's lying on her side, has an enormous gash tearing it open, a gash so deep that... God. Is that a bit of *bone* I see, peeking through the layers of skin and muscle? Blood leaks down her side, coursing over her arm, over her chest, pooling onto the floor beneath her.

Her long, wavy, brunette hair is obscuring her face, but I can tell—obviously—that she's a woman. I can see the curve of her breasts past her arms, can see the curve of her hips. But everything is moving too fast for me to compute what I'm seeing. I reach out to her, my hand pausing above her bare arm, not yet touching her, because I stop myself just in time. She's really hurt; I don't want to hurt her even further. I can't possibly tell what other injuries she's sustained.

"Are you okay?" I ask her, breathless, realizing after I say it that it's *the stupidest question in the universe*. She's naked, bleeding, in the middle of a campground bathroom. She is very much *not* okay. Obviously.

But when she lifts her head to glance up at me from her position on the floor, when her hair falls away from her face, I'm made breathless again, as if all the air has left my body.

I stare at her, speechless.

Her eyes are brown; they *have* to be brown. That's the only thing that makes any sort of sense to me. I've seen a million women with brown eyes, even brown eyes framed with such lovely lashes as she has. Brown eyes make *sense*.

But the truth of the matter is that her eyes *aren't* brown.

They're...golden. Like, pure gold, fine gold, the type of gold that you find in a jewelry store or in a museum, something precious. Her eyes are that bright, burnished gold, with flecks of amber sprinkled throughout to create a sense that an all-consuming fire is burning in her eyes.

And she's aiming that fire directly into me, holding my gaze with such bright, fevered, fiery eyes that I'm rendered breathless.

"You," she growls, and her voice is low, husky, as deep as her eyes, as she stares up at me from the ground. "...shouldn't," she manages, coughing a little as she curls further inward. "Be here," she finishes, closing her eyes in pain as she presses her face again to her knees, her body clenched up into such a tight ball that I can see the muscles on her arms flexing as she draws her legs closer to her chest.

"Can I... Can I help you?" I ask her in a hushed voice, my heart pounding in my throat as I stare down at the blood spilling out of the wound on her shoulder now that the muscle is tighter. "You need help," I finally manage to tell her.

Again, she opens her eyes. Again, she lifts up her face from the floor, turning that burning, golden gaze onto me. Her full lips are curled up into a grimace, and her eyes are narrowed as she winces, as she shakes her head tiredly.

"Please go," she tells me softly, her voice low, a growl. "You could get hurt," she says, and then she hisses in pain, reaching up, curling her fingers over the wound as she moans. "Please," she growls again, and she pushes herself to a sitting position, her arms crossed in front of her, her one hand gripping the edges of her wound so that they press together as she gasps out loud from the pain. She stops, then, her mouth open as she practically pants, staring at me with pain-filled eyes, her gaze burning like a fever.

"You aren't safe here," she murmurs to me, enunciating each word with a growling precision as she leans forward a little, as she holds my gaze with her unnatural golden eyes. And then, across the space between us, she takes her hand, the hand not covered in blood, the hand not closed tightly over the wound in her shoulder—and she reaches out to me.

I'm so shocked that I remain perfectly still. Her fingers are feather-light on my cheek as she brushes aside one of the strands of wet hair that's dripping on my face, my shoulders. She smooths the pads of her fingers delicately over my skin—even as her hand shakes, even as she gasps from the pain of her wound.

She presses her hot skin against mine, and she keeps her hand there, her palm gently cupping my face. She holds my gaze unwaveringly.

"I will not," she growls, her eyes sparking, "see another person get hurt by her," she tells me, gasping now as she forces out the words, her voice guttural. "You. Must. Leave."

"Someone... Someone hurt you?" I ask her, not understanding. I'm feeling a million things at the moment, a million emotions vying for supremacy inside of me, but here's the one that came up instantly, burning through me just as brightly as fire:

Longing. Longing so intense, so immediate, so fierce, that I'm made breathless by it, as breathless as if I've fallen onto my back, as if every last bit of air has been knocked out of me.

Something awakened when the woman reached out to touch me. There's something in her touch that ignites me, burning deep inside of me. Something that opens, unfurling, like the woman uncurling from the tight ball of pain on the concrete floor. Yes. Unfurling is the best word for what happened inside of my heart just now.

But...but...I would be the *first* one to point out that *now is not the time for this sort of thing*. Really, Abby? You're going to go all doe-eyed for a woman who's lying in front of you, probably *bleeding to death*? But I can't *help* the immediate reaction, this visceral reaction, that I have to her reaching out to touch my face, the deep reaction that I have to her bright, golden eyes pinning me in place, the reaction that I have to the electric heat of her skin against mine.

I have never, in all of my life, felt that sort of connection to anyone. It's... Well, it's genuinely *unnerving*, how quickly those feelings rear up inside of me, how quickly I am attracted to this woman, this woman who is bleeding in front of me. So I do my absolute best to push all of that desire down, shoving it away as the woman in front of me gasps again, curling her fingers tighter over the wound in her shoulder. She crumples forward, and her fingers leave my face, because she can no longer hold herself up by the strength of her core. She curves forward elegantly, in so much obvious pain that the sight guts me.

She's bleeding to death in front of me, and I don't even know her name.

"I need to get you some help," I whisper, standing, shaking like I've just seen a ghost. But I haven't seen a ghost; I saw a wolf (that obviously wasn't there. Obviously. Yeah, I'm going to go with that), and then I saw a woman wounded, bleeding, needing my help.

So I stand, and I rush over to the bench, throwing on my old jeans and fleece jacket over my bare shoulders, zipping it up with trembling hands. They're shaking so hard, in fact, that it takes me a few tries to grasp the zipper and pull it up and over my abdomen and breasts. I grab my phone out of my purse, slide the screen to unlock it and dial in the number that you hope you never have to call: 911.

I hold the phone up to my ear, but because Allegany State Park is absolutely notorious for bad signals, the phone call doesn't go through. There's no phone reception here in the bathroom. I stare down at my cell, dumbstruck. Why wouldn't it work now? When I seriously need it most? I know that cell service is completely reliable in the park, but this woman is *going to die.*

Don't ask me how I know that. It's not like I've ever seen a dying woman before. But there's something about the way that she looked at me, with those feverish, bright eyes, that convinced me that there was something very, very wrong. I don't know what she's talking about: she said, "I will not see another person get hurt by her." I have no idea what that could possibly mean, but my mind is already jumping to all sorts of terrible conclusions. Maybe this woman was kidnapped, and she just escaped from her kidnapper? Why is she naked? None of this makes any *sense*.

I groan in frustration as I toss my phone back into my purse, turning to look back at the woman, who is now on all fours, folding forward as she moans with pain.

"I'm sorry," I tell her, rummaging around in my pack with shaking hands. I grab out the robe that I was going to wear in the cabin after the shower (yeah, I may be one of the only people who brings a robe on a camping trip, but I wanted to be comfortable on my vacation, dammit!), and I bring it over to her, hovering back, unsure as she glances up at me.

"Um...here..." I tell her, offering it to her. She

glances up at me with those same burning, bright eyes, and she nods once, grunting as she pushes off the floor with her hands, pushing herself up to a kneeling position on the concrete, her shoulders bowing forward, her head lowered as she grits her teeth, staring down and taking short, panting breaths.

"Thank you," she finally growls to me, reaching up and taking the robe from my hands. The robe falls to the floor as she grips it tightly with white-knuckled fingers, her fist sinking to the ground as she presses against it, letting out a low grunt of pain. Then she rises a little, gingerly slinging the robe over her good shoulder, and then gasping out again as she draws the fabric up and over her wound. She cries out as she slides her right arm into the arm hole, and then she draws the robe closed in front of her with shaking hands, tying the terrycloth sash with stiff fingers.

She places one hand on the ground again, palm flat against the cool concrete, and she lifts her right knee. For a long moment, she crouches in this position, like she's down on one knee before me, her head bent, her shining brown hair falling over her shoulders, the curve of her neck visible beneath the curls... I gulp down air and try not to stare at her, but then she leans forward, gasping, and in one slow, stiff motion, she pushes herself up to a standing position.

But she's not ready to stand yet; she's either lost too much blood, or she's hurt far worse than I can see, because as she stands there, wavering, she begins to fold forward.

"Oh, my gosh," I manage, darting toward her as she sags, about to fall back onto the concrete floor in an uncontrolled dive. I grab her, throwing an arm around her waist, drawing my other hand up to grip her left hand. It looks like we're about to start tangoing, really, as she falls against me, pillowing her head on my shoulder.

"I just... I just need a minute," she growls out softly, and her breath is hot on my ear as she closes her eyes, sagging, her long, dark lashes fluttering against her pale cheeks. And I'm left holding her up.

She's taller than me, that much is obvious, even though she can't exactly stand upright right now of her own volition, and she's curvy and muscular, so she's also heavier than me. It's all I can do to hold her in place, but I manage, gripping her around her waist now, holding tightly to her.

I'm highly aware in this moment of so many things at once, and some of these things I shouldn't even be *thinking* about, but I can't help it. Because I notice, acutely, how her curving breasts are pressing against me through the robe, how the silky curves of her hips grind against mine as she gasps out, how her wound is leaking blood onto my fleece jacket, actually *dripping* down my shoulder, the blood running over the waterproof fleece fabric to *drip, drip* down onto the concrete floor.

I grimace, wrapping my arms tighter around her waist as she starts to slip. Okay, *think,* Abby! First things first. I've got to get her to my car. And from there...I guess to the hospital? I can't call an ambulance, and by the time I do get a signal... I don't know. It might be too late for her.

I've got to get her to the hospital *now*.

I do some quick math in my head as I grip her tightly, her long, curving body resting completely against mine. The closest hospital is Olean General. I remember this because of that one time when I was ten, and we were camping here for the summer, and my cousin, Brett, dared me to climb the tallest of the Thunder Rocks in the park, and I unfortunately fell off (it *would* have been my greatest climb to date!) and broke my wrist. My mother drove me, cursing all the way, to the hospital. But even though Olean is "close" in relative terms, it's still *forty minutes away*. Maybe even more, because of how far into the park we are.

This woman, this stranger, is bleeding out on me. What if she dies before we even *get* there?

She's hardly conscious, but she makes a guttural sound now, like the sound a wild animal would make when it's in pain. She lifts her head up from my shoulder, her brow furrowed, her eyes bright with torment.

"What are you doing?" she mutters, gazing at me, her mouth open, her lips wet as she pants against me. I swallow a little, take a deep breath.

"Um...my phone isn't working right now," I tell her miserably, "and you're very hurt. I'm sorry. My phone can't call 911, but I can keep trying—but I thought I'd try to drive you to the hospital. You're very hurt," I repeat, muttering the words as she closes her bright golden eyes tightly.

She pushes against me, but it's a weak push. She shakes her head vehemently, her eyes burning even brighter as she opens them, as she pins me to the spot with the power of her gaze. "No," she tells me, the word hushed but forceful. "I can't go to the hospital. I just... I really can't," she says, and she's pushing out the words so fast now, breathless as she gasps in pain. "Just... You've been kind," she says, holding my gaze as she grips my shoulders tightly with her fingers, using them to help her stand up straight. "But I have to go.

Someone..." She trails off, shaking her head, as if trying to clear cobwebs from her mind. "Someone is expecting me," she tells me, glancing backward at the door, her hair falling over her good shoulder with a soft *shushing* sound. Everything sounds too loud in the stillness of the bathroom now, as I hold her, as her fingers curl around my shoulders.

I can hear her breathing. I can practically hear her heart beating.

"You have a serious injury," I tell her then, and she takes a step back from me, no longer touching me but hardly standing up on her own. She can't support herself yet, and she stumbles a little as she takes that first step. She's about to fall to the concrete again, but I'm gasping, leaping forward, gripping her around the waist in a second. She was about to fall to her knees very hard before I caught her, my arms wrapping around her body tightly, like a lover might hold someone.

But she's holding me close, too, as she draws her arms around my shoulders then, gazing into my eyes with her face so close that her nose actually brushes against mine. Her mouth is so very, *very* close to mine. She gazes at me, her eyes intense and burning, the scent of her rising around me—of forest pine and rich earth and a million fallen leaves... She smells wild, I realize. As wild as the wood.

I realize, then, in this moment, how very close she is...and how easy it would be to kiss her.

For that hot, searing second, I let myself think about that, let myself imagine exactly what that might be like...but then the shame rises in me, instantaneous and painful. Shame that I would even have that thought as this poor woman bleeds against me. She needs my *help*, and here I am thinking of kissing her, even as the blood leaks out of her shoulder, pouring over my fleece jacket... God, I really need to get my head on straight.

The problem is that everything changes too quickly in me, and in that moment, I really don't even know if I'm coming or going—because that shame I just felt, that red, hot shame that pulsed through me because I dared think about this woman's kiss... Well, that shame rushes out of me in a heartbeat, evaporating like it was never there.

It is, instead, replaced with something vastly different.

Because this woman, this perfect stranger who I didn't know more than a handful of moments ago, leans forward. She erases the distance between us. Her nose brushes past mine, and then she places her feverishly hot, full mouth against my cheek.

My heart thunders through me, and I can feel my blood beating loudly, rushing through every vein of my body as she kisses my skin, her cheek pressed against my own, her mouth kissing me softly, hotly, every bit of attention I have zeroed in on that single inch of skin.

She lingers for a long moment before she leans forward a little more, and her mouth is at my ear. "You have been kind," she repeats, whispering the words, her breath hot against me. I blush brightly. I can feel her lips against my earlobe, and it's so sensual, so soft and smooth, this motion, like we were lovers once, like we could be lovers again... This degree of intimacy is not reserved for someone you've just met.

But she draws me to her, and something is tightening around my heart, squeezing it as she squeezes me gently.

I turn to her because I must turn to her, because I am drawn to her in a way I don't understand.

She sighs, and then she whispers, "But you must let me go. You are not safe here."

And then she squeezes me gently one last time and takes a step back from me.

And I'm so surprised by the fact that she kissed me that I just stand there, my arms loose, in shock...and I let her go.

The woman glances around the bathroom now, her golden eyes shrewd, calculating, as she takes in everything, as she reaches up, pressing her hand against her wounded shoulder again, almost absentmindedly. My robe *was* bright white, but now the shoulder and the right arm are completely saturated with blood, leaking through the fabric in a bright red color that stands out starkly against the drab gray of the concrete floors and badly-painted mauve of the bathroom walls. She's staring at the wall closest to us now, and her head is tilting softly to the side, her eyes narrowing, her wet mouth parted...

It's almost as if she's...listening for something.

I realize that I'm reaching up to place my hand over my heart as she turns to me then, her eyes still narrowed, still calculating.

"You're alone in here, yes?" she asks me, her voice low, soft, and again, I shiver because I have no idea what this poor woman has been through. I nod, though.

"Yes. I'm alone," I tell her, wrapping my arms around myself. "Just...please..." I begin, because something deep inside of me is aching. She looks so hurt, so vulnerable, and like she's not used to being either one of those things. "Please let me help you?" I ask her, my voice soft, too.

She glances back at me as she grips her shoulder, as she takes a deep breath, her nostrils flaring. Her eyes are softer when they gaze at me, but the fire that seems to burn, never-ending, deep inside of her flares a little as she looks me up and down now. Her gaze is lingering as it travels the full length of my body.

"I'm glad it was you," she finally says, her eyes landing back on my own, her mouth curling up at the corners, just a little. "That you were here," she says, gesturing around us, at the bathroom that she now finds herself in. "That you were kind," she whispers.

And then she takes two very sure steps forward. These steps are enough to bring her right back to me, her breasts pressing against me just like they had a few moments ago when I was holding her up. But I'm not holding her up anymore. I stare at her in shock as she wraps her free hand, the hand not gripping her wound, around my middle, drawing me to her.

"Thank you," she murmurs again, searching my eyes. "Do you mind?" she asks me then, and though her face is still pained, one brow raises, and she gazes down at my lips with a small smirk.

I have no idea what she's even talking about, but I shake my head—no, I don't mind—not realizing what I'm agreeing to.

But then I realize what she was asking. Because the woman leans forward, and she does not lean down to brush her lips against my cheek. No: instead, she captures my mouth with her own.

She's bleeding. I can feel the wetness of her shoulder pressing against mine as she leans down, but everything else, including the fact that she's terribly wounded, seems to disappear as she holds me tightly to her and kisses me with an intensity and fierceness that undoes me.

Her mouth is so hot, just like her skin, hot to the touch but not unpleasantly so, as I tilt my face up and I realize in that surprising moment that I am kissing her back. I'm made breathless by the intoxicating quality of her kiss, of her skin against mine, of her body against mine, every curve of hers fitting against mine seamlessly. She tastes like she smells, of the crisp, cold outdoors, of a sweet pine, of a cold, bright mint that reminds me of winter nights under countless stars. The coolness of the mint and the heat of her mouth combine in this bewitching play of cold and hot that feels utterly delicious against my mouth. She is *such* a good kisser, I think, as she sucks my lower lip, as she darts her tongue into my mouth expertly. I haven't been kissed like this in...well...a long time.

And I don't want it to end.

But, just as quickly, she's stepping back, that small smile growing a little more as she shakes her head, her face rueful.

"I apologize," she tells me in that low growl, though her sideways smile is telling me she's not sorry in the slightest. "I saw you looking at me, and I made an assumption. I hope... I hope I have not offended you." And she looks sincere when she says this, her brow furrowed, her smile fading.

"Um," I tell her, still speechless, but trying very, very hard to activate the putting-sentences-together part of my brain again. "No, no, you didn't offend me," I tell her quickly, stammering. "I...I liked that." Inwardly, I bang my head against the stupid mauve walls. That sounded like something a twelve-year-old boy would say. Great. Real smooth, Abby.

But this stranger doesn't seem to notice my lack of suaveness. She's staring at me with her intense gaze, pinning me in place. "It's just that, tonight..." she murmurs, searching my eyes. "I could lose everything tonight. Even my life," she says, her voice solemn and quiet as the smile fades from her face. "I needed something soft," she whispers, her gaze trailing down to my lips with a heat that sparks desire through every vein inside of me. "Thank you for that last kindness," she tells me softly, her eyes lingering on my mouth.

But then she turns slowly, with purpose, and she heads toward the door, her legs stiff as she walks proudly, walking away from me.

What?

What the hell does she mean, that she could lose her *life*?

This woman, this perfect stranger, is about to leave the building, about to slip away into that darkness. But she's hurt, and she's bleeding, and she just kissed me.

And I don't even know her name.

"Wait!" I call after her, breathless. Her hand is already on the door; it's cracked open, the cold night air spilling into the bathroom. But she pauses, glancing back at me, her brown hair sweeping over her shoulder as she gazes at me with her warm golden eyes. She stands there, holding that door open, and she tilts her chin up, watching me.

I want to tell her a lot of things right now. I want to reiterate that I want to help her, that she could come to my cabin; I could drive her to the hospital, could try calling 911 again. I want to ask her if she's in trouble, if someone is after her, if there is anything I can do to help. I want to tell her that I will do anything to help her. Because, in that moment, I realize that I will.

But I can't get any of that out, find that I can't even make a single sound come out of my mouth. It doesn't matter, because one foot is being placed in front of the other, and I'm tugged across the room toward her, like there's a bright ribbon between us, and it's pulling tighter, tightening, drawing us together.

Every single thing about this night has been strange, from the deer bounding out in front of me (I've been coming here since childhood and have never had a run-in with a deer), to Barbara practically threatening me, to finding a wolf in the middle of the bathroom floor—but then not really. Instead, I found a naked woman. And she kissed me. A stranger *kissed* me, and I don't know if it's pathetic to say this, but it's been a *long* time since another woman I was deeply attracted to kissed me passionately, so recklessly...like she had nothing to lose.

So even though my cheeks are probably bright red, and—more importantly—even though this perfect stranger is still bleeding through the fabric of my robe, and even though she was just about to leave...

I find that I don't want her to.

I cross that space between us, and I put my hands tentatively at the curves of her waist, over the robe's fabric. The woman lets the door shut behind her gently, and the cold air is cut off. She glances down at me, her head a little to the side as she watches me. And I stand up, tilting my head back, breathless.

And I kiss her, too.

Her mouth is smiling against me when we touch, when my mouth slowly, gently, tenuously, covers hers. My mouth opens, and the kiss is suddenly hot, hotter, as the heat from her skin and body begins to overtake how cold I am after stepping out of that shower and being naked on the concrete floor.

Why isn't *she* cold?

But thoughts like that, normal thoughts, thoughts that make *sense*, are out of place in this moment, on this very strange night. Because I need to be honest: absolutely *none* of this makes sense right now, and yet I'm still going with it.

Because I want to.

Because I need to.

She's hot against me, her skin blazing with pure heat against mine, her mouth everything I didn't know I wanted, but wanted so much that to have it now undoes me. I need her, I realize, as I wrap an arm around her neck, as my body stretches against hers, reaching up for something so wonderful as this kiss that is happening between us. I need her.

Wow... This escalated fast, I realize, as I press my body against hers, as I feel the curve of her breasts against me through the robe and my fleece, as I feel my own chest pressing against hers, as I wrap my fingers around her hips, pulling her to me. I wasn't expecting this tonight, but something about the fact that this is so out of the blue, so unexpected and out of the ordinary, pushes all the right buttons inside of me.

But I back up for a moment, lean back, search her eyes, full of need but so confused...

She's injured, and she's injured *terribly*.

I know that she's kissing me back; I know that her eyes are dark with desire... But I can't possibly be doing this. She's *injured*.

Still, there's that equal need in her eyes, and as I

look at her kissed lips, how swollen they are from my ministrations, how flashing her eyes are with desire, darkening as they stare at me, I flick my gaze to her shoulder, just to see how it is...

And then I freeze, staring at her shoulder.

This...can't possibly be happening.

My breathing starts to speed up again, my heart pounding even harder through me as I reach up, running my fingers under the lapel of the robe, pulling it aside, sliding it over her shoulder...

Yes, my robe is saturated with blood. It's stiff, because the blood on the cloth is already drying, and her skin is slick with the stuff. But when I pull the robe aside, the cloth slides over perfect, unmarred skin.

Where there is not a single trace of a wound.

I glance at her then, my brow furrowed, my mouth open, my breath coming fast. "What..." I whisper, but she stays me before I can take another step, her hand at the small of my back, firm and gentle—but unyielding.

"Don't go," she whispers, her eyes sparking as she licks her lips, as she lets her gaze drift down my face, down my neck, further, her eyes darkening more until they are no longer golden but a rich, deep amber. Her breaths come faster, and I feel the press of her fingers at my back, pulling me closer.

"Please," she murmurs, her head to the side, a small smile turning her mouth up at the corners as she holds my gaze. "I...I have to be somewhere tonight," she tells me softly, voice low, "but...I have some time right now." She blinks slowly, cat-like, her mouth curved in a secretive smile. "If you'll have me."

Wait a second... Is she saying what I think she's saying?

But I can't get over her miraculously healed shoulder.

That just isn't possible.

"What... What in the *world*..." I whisper to her, staring at her, my breath coming fast, almost panting now as I lean back in her arms, pushing away a little. "You had... I could see a bit of your *bone*. You had this terrible wound..."

With one arm still around my waist, she shimmies her shoulders, and the robe slips off both of them, falling down to the tie still wrapped tightly around her waist. Her shoulders, her arms, her perfect breasts, her abdomen...it's all in front of me, all bare, all exposed, and though the curve of her right shoulder is coated with dried blood, it is very, very easy to see: there's not a bit of unevenness in her skin, not a wound, not a cut. Hell, there's not even a tiny *scratch* there.

"Yes, I was hurt," she tells me with maddening patience, "but I'm...better," she says succinctly, her eyes sparkling as her smirk deepens. And then she doesn't say anything else. She only leans close to me and kisses me.

Did I imagine that wolf in the middle of the room? I mean, I must have. I don't know how, but I *must* have, because the wolf wasn't in the room anymore when I looked again, peering out from around that shower curtain... Instead, there was this woman lying in the middle of the floor. This woman, bleeding out of a wound on her shoulder...

A wound she no longer *has*.

I'm incredibly confused, but she's standing here, flesh and blood, and she's absolutely, one hundred percent *real* as she kisses me as if I'm the last woman on

51

Earth, as if we're all alone on the planet. I *like* how she's kissing me like there's no tomorrow, like this moment together is all we have. I'm powerfully attracted to her, and the feeling seems to be mutual.

But...what about the blood, the wound?

I don't know what to do. I just... I *don't know what to do*. But as she stands there, her warm hands at my waist, drawing me to her, her breasts pressed against the front of my jacket, the curves of her skin a feast for my senses, it is alarmingly easy for me to relax against her, relax and put my arms up and around her shoulders and kiss her back.

I'm hungry, I'm tired, I'm dismayed at how strange things have been, but I've seemingly plowed through all of these facts. We stand together, and she holds me tightly, her fingers now digging into my hips; she's gripping me with such strength. And as she holds me, I feel everything so deeply, every tiny physical sensation, from the way that her mouth curls up at the corners, smiling against me as I kiss her, to the way that her curved belly feels against my own, to the way that her arm muscles flex when I reach up, when I curl my own fingers over her upper arm, delighting in the feel of her hot skin beneath my palm...

I wonder.

I wonder if I imagined the wound, too.

This is all distressing. It's genuinely scary to think that I could imagine something so terrifying as a wolf in the center of a bathroom, and a woman's wound. There's so much blood, I couldn't possibly have imagined it...

So, yes, I want to keep kissing her. But I find that I just can't.

I pull back from her, albeit reluctantly, and the

woman stands there, her full mouth wet, swollen. She's beautiful as she stares at me with hooded eyes, eyes that reflect how very much she wants me.

A shiver runs through me—I want her, too—but I take a deep breath.

"What's going on?" I ask her then, my voice soft as I stare into her impossible golden eyes. "Who are you?" I finally manage. "I...I don't even know your name."

For a long moment, she says nothing, only taking long, deep breaths as she looks at me. But then she nods, her gaze softening. "My name is Shannon," she tells me, flexing her fingers at my waist. "And what's yours?"

"Abby," I tell her, swallowing a little. "Abigail Reynolds."

"Well, Abby," she says, taking up my right hand. She brings my hand to her heart and flattens my palm against her bare skin. I shiver a little as I feel the *thump-thump* of her heartbeat beneath my palm, also shivering at the smooth softness of her breast beneath my hand. Shannon holds my gaze with eyes that are full of softness, yes. But they are also full of need as she breathes out. "Do you trust me?" she whispers then.

What an impossible question. I just met her. She was bleeding, completely naked. I don't know who she is, where she's from, or what's going on. Where did she get that wound from? *Why* was she naked?

What could possibly be happening here?

But I realize, as I hold my palm over her heart, as I feel that heartbeat beneath my skin, feel that heartbeat deep in my bones, that—as odd as it sounds—I *do* trust her.

I don't know why. I couldn't tell you why if you asked me. Maybe it's the look she gives me, like she already knows me, has always known me. Maybe it's because I feel like I've always known her, too, but in such a different way. Maybe it's because, from the very first moment I set my eyes on her, it felt like we were, in some odd way, connected, the two of us.

I do trust her.

So I lick my lips; I clear my throat.

And I find myself nodding.

"Yes," I tell her, holding her gaze, feeling my heartbeat intensify as she watches me with those unnerving, beautiful eyes. "I...I trust you."

My hand is still against her heart, and it's pressed harder against it when Shannon steps closer. She bends her head, her neck curving beautifully, her hair falling over her shoulder as she meets me in a kiss.

It's a slow, sensual kiss this time. She takes her time, her mouth open, hot, searing, as she tastes me, dragging her tongue over my lips as she begins to move with more fervor.

My hands are at her waist, and I'm undoing the tie to my own robe that's wrapped tightly around her as I fumble with the sash, trying to get the tight knot, stiffened with her dry blood, undone.

For half a heartbeat, that dry blood, crumbling from the fabric onto my fingers, shoves me right out of the moment, but then the tie comes loose, and Shannon seems to have an idea about how to distract me.

She pulls me, still kissing me, toward the showers.

When we step inside the first one, past the curtain, I fumble over her shoulder and turn on the knobs, and we are instantly awash in hot water that pummels us with a heat so profound I wonder if we're going to get burned by it. But I fumble a little more with the cold water knob, my eyes closed, my other arm wrapped tightly around her neck and shoulders, and then the water is a little less boil-you-alive, though still very hot.

And Shannon presses me up against the back concrete wall.

I gasp, a sound that gets lost in the roar of the water as I tilt my head back, as Shannon kisses my neck, her mouth hot and open against skin that she teases with her tongue and teeth. Her one hand is at my hips, but the other is under my right thigh then, and she's lifting it, drawing it up to her hips so that I wrap my leg around her curve, and I gasp again, panting against her, as her wet fingers draw hot lines along the skin of that thigh.

I curl my fingers in her hair, pulling her back up to my mouth, because I need to kiss her at this moment. Every touch feels so good, but this is all so strange: if she's not right here, right now, if she's not kissing me fiercely, I'm going to go into my head, even though she's setting me on fire.

And I don't want to be in my head. I don't want to think about the million strange things of this night, the million things that don't make sense.

I want to forget about all of them. I want to be right here. Right now.

With her.

Shannon seems to sense this, because her movements, her touches, were starting to get quicker, full of wanting, but she backs off now, back to a slow, sensual seduction as she captures my mouth, as she teases me with her tongue, parting my lips, pressing into my mouth. I gasp against her, my fingers wrapped up in her wet curls as I draw her head down to me, tightening my leg around her hip, straining, pushing so that my center can feel some release, moving against her.

Shannon reaches up, her fingers on the zipper pull of my fleece jacket, and she tugs it down. I wasn't wearing anything underneath, so she pulls the rest of the thing off, over my shoulders and arms, until it settles into a wet puddle on the floor of the shower. She also undoes my fly with a single, practiced hand, and then she's tugging the jeans off, over my hips, and they, too, form a sodden mass at my feet as I kick them away.

She holds my gaze as she presses me against the wall again, as she picks me up, hooking her arms under my thighs, settling my legs around her waist.

And she presses her hips against me hard, grinding them against my center.

"Oh, my God," I whisper, my head rolling back, my eyes closing as I gasp, as that exquisite sensation of her hot, wet skin against mine causes my eyes to roll back in my head, causes my body to arch, of its own accord, against her own. My legs are so widespread because she has me pressed against the wall, and that sensation is exquisite as she begins to slowly—at first—and rhythmically grind her hips, pulsing her center against mine.

The friction is delicious; the sensation of her hands, long fingers beneath my thighs, causes every single inch of my skin to come alive. She bends low, capturing my left nipple in her mouth, and she doesn't wait to savor anything. She doesn't tease me. She bites.

It's exactly what I need, and somehow, she seems to know that. It's sensual enough that it doesn't hurt, but it's almost at the threshold of pain. With perfect pressure, she uses her tongue to press my nipple against her teeth, flicking it, sucking at it. Both of my nipples are straining, peaked and hard, and she seems to know exactly what she's doing to me as she glances up at me from where she is, bending low to tease me, with such a beautiful smirk.

The water pummels us, raining down on my head, sliding over my shoulders, my breasts, with intoxicating heat, as Shannon bends low again and gives these same ministrations to my right breast. She starts by tracing her tongue up and over the curve of my breast, at the same time that her right hand leaves my right thigh. I still have my leg hooked over her hip, and I keep it there, even as her fingertips trace up and over my skin. She rounds the top of my thigh, and then she dips her hand between us, making space for her arm, just as she takes my right nipple in her mouth.

She bites down, hard, and she slides her slick fingers over my clit.

I gasp out against her, bucking my hips as she slides her fingers, with absolutely no resistance, deep inside of me. She starts with two, but it's obvious that I can take more, and can take more quickly, because she's adding a third as I moan, pressing the back of my head to the wall, gripping her shoulders so tightly with my fingernails that I'm going to leave red crescent moons in her skin...

She gives me short, hard strokes, her thumb sliding over my clit each time she enters me, the heel of her hand pressing hard against it each time she rhythmically strokes in and out. It is exquisite, exactly the right pressure, with a finesse that makes me gasp, makes me cry out unintelligibly.

The water sliding over us, the touch of her teeth against me, how she licks and teases my neck, finally capturing my mouth with hers again, consumes me. I feel everything, the heat of that water, the press of her fingers against my thigh, the way she curves her fingers inside of me, thrusting up and in, using her hips to press her wrist hard against my center, the pressure utterly intoxicating.

The orgasm that hits me then is surprising in its ferocity as I tilt my head back, as I gasp, my entire body transcendent. She presses into me with such intensity that it draws the orgasm out, out, out, and every inch of my skin is shivering from the experience. My legs are quaking as she draws the crescendo out until the very last second...and then she stops. Her wrist no longer presses against me, and she pulls her fingers out of me slowly, softly, almost reverently.

She curves her hands around both of my thighs now as I lean against her, my head pillowed on her shoulder. I wrap my arms around her neck, feeling every last inch of me against every last inch of her.

I take a deep breath, want still pulsing through me, pulsing in time to the aftershocks of that exquisite orgasm. That want should be sated, but it's not. Because I want to feel her beneath my hands, beneath my mouth. *I* want to feel *her*.

I push off a little from the wall and slide my legs down hers until my shaky feet rest against the ground again. Then I glance up at her, give her a small smile as the hot water continues to pummel us, and I reach up, standing on my shaky toes, wrapping my arms tightly around her neck. And I kiss her.

This kiss is slow, a dance of tongues as I taste her, as I lick her and tease her, my kiss leaving her mouth and tracing down the curve of her strong chin. I kiss her neck, feel her jaw clench against me as I trail my fingernails down her front, over the outside curve of her right breast, over her ribs and down to her stomach. She doesn't make a single sound as I reach up again, taking her right nipple in my fingers, twisting it softly.

Then harder, as I watch her, as my other hand draws nails down, over her left thigh.

Finally, she gasps against my hand as I pull and pluck and tease that nipple, and I smile against her as I lean down, taking her left nipple in my mouth. Like she bit mine, I bite hers, teasing with my teeth, again starting very slowly, sensually, softly, building up the pressure of my love bites harder and harder until she's gasping against me, wrapping her fingers in my hair and pressing me down, harder, against her breast.

I oblige, sucking hard at her nipple, then biting down again. She hisses out, ending with a moan, as I wrap my fingers around her hips, digging in with my nails. I turn and press her back against the wall, too.

And then I crouch down smoothly, the water running over me with the same force as a waterfall. I stare up at the gorgeous woman leaning against the wall above me.

She looks down at me with eyes full of desire, her hands still in my hair. I have my head to the side. A question. Can I? I'm crouching in front of her, my fingers digging into her hips; there is only one question I could possibly be asking. And she nods, biting her lip, pushing against my head gently with her fingers.

Yes, yes, yes. All she is is yes as I lean forward, onto my knees, as I trail my fingers down to the insides of her thighs, gently pushing her legs wider, opening them to me.

And I lean forward all the way, lifting up my face as I press a kiss to her clit.

She shudders against me as I flick my tongue out, as I taste her. It is decadent, the taste of her, musky and sweet and everything I crave as I curve the fingers of my right hand around, touching her center, twisting my fingers as I feel her wetness, pressing up as I press my head forward, as she pushes down on it with her hands, asking, begging with her fingers that twist tighter in my hair.

So I answer her wants with my own. I taste her as the water washes over us; I taste her wetness, electricity crackling inside of me as I realize exactly how wet she is, as my fingers drift over her center. I tease her for a long moment, nudging a knuckle against her opening, but then I can't take it anymore: I want to feel her against me. So slowly, reverently, I turn my hand, curl my fingers up and inside of her.

I move in and out of her at first slowly, but eventually, I build up the rhythmic pace until she's bucking her hips against my mouth, against my hand.

Her taste, the velvet softness of her against my mouth, is a thrill that races through every vein inside of me, my skin hot, electric, as I touch her, as I taste her. The musky wildness of her taste is something that I am going to crave, I realize, as my tongue moves against her, as my fingers feel inside of her.

I am going to crave this again.

I can feel her pulse around my fingers right before she moans, long and low, above me, and then I can feel the orgasm moving against my hand, can feel her entire body pulsing against me as she comes.

I lick her slower, then, drawing my tongue over her clit very, very slowly as I try to play her like a musical instrument, as I try to draw the orgasm out of her for as long as possible. And only when she's shaking against me do I stop, her fingers slack in my hair now, her body loose-limbed and relaxed, as she leans against the wall, as she glances down at me with a slow, lazy smile, tugging my hair a little as she draws me back up her body. I lick my lips as I come up and out of the crouch, and I press my body against her as she smiles against me, wrapping her arms around my neck and shoulders, drawing me to her for a kiss.

She tastes herself on me, because she licks my lips, my chin, drinking it all in as she kisses me fiercely then.

For a long moment, we stay just like that, locked in this warm embrace, weak and spent and so deeply sated...but then the water is starting to turn lukewarm, and bracing cold is next on the agenda, so I take a small step back from her, and I wipe my wet hands up and over my face, giving it a good scrub in the water, before glancing back at her. She nods, and I turn the knobs off.

And then we're standing there, the both of us, wet and naked and utterly sated. She laughs a little, stepping forward, wrapping her arms around me again, her front pressing against mine, her breasts against me, her hips against me. Everything feels so good as she kisses me again softly, slowly.

"You're delicious," Shannon whispers to me, letting her lips find my earlobe and sucking on it gently before she kisses my cheek almost chastely, her mouth closed. She then takes a step back, her mouth curling up at the corners mischievously. "Thanks for that," she tells me, as she slicks her hands over her hair, letting the waves fall over her shoulders as she shakes her head, still smiling softly at me.

But then she sighs out, and though her eyes are still sparking with fire, it's more subdued now. "I...I guess I'll be seeing you," she tells me, almost regretfully, as she steps out of the shower.

"What?" I ask, blinking after her, but then I scoop up my sopping wet jeans and fleece jacket, and I follow out after her, into the searingly bright bathroom hallway.

"You're just going to...just going to leave? Just like that?" I ask her, spluttering, staring at her gorgeous backside as she walks away from me. She stops, turns, taking me in, too, and she smiles appreciatively at me.

"I have someplace to be," she tells me with a small shrug, though her eyes are, again, regretful.

"But...you need clothes," I point out to her, gesturing to her nude body. "You can't waltz like that out into the woods. You'll catch your death."

"I assure you," she tells me, her mouth twitching upward at the corners, "I'll be fine."

"You just can't go out into the woods like that," I tell her again, and it sounds like I'm pleading with her, and that grates on me. But what we just did meant something to me. And I don't want her to disappear.

I'm not a love-'em-and-leave-'em kind of girl. And I'm trying not to be clingy, but was that it? What about the connection I feel with her?

What about, "Do you trust me?"

She turns back to me, hands on her hips, chin lifted, her chest rising and falling as she breathes. And as I stand there, as I take in her commanding presence, I'm made breathless by her physique, her breasts, the swell of her hips. Every curve she possesses draws me to her, like a magnet. I realize, as I'm staring at her, that I've been looking for this woman my whole life, and never knew exactly how much I wanted to find her.

Her golden eyes flash with bemusement as she catches my gaze roving over her body. "Well...do you have clothes?" she asks me, her head to the side as she assesses my body, too, partly because she seemingly likes to look at it and partly—I think—to gauge my size. "I don't know if I'd fit in them. I'm bigger than you," she says, gesturing to her height, "but if you'd let me borrow some..."

"Yes!" I say quickly, then gulp down air and smile a little self-consciously. "I mean, I don't have them with me... I have towels here," I tell her, gesturing to my pack, "that you could wrap around yourself, and I have one change of clothes for me, but everything else is in my car."

She nods, glancing to my pack. "Well," she tells me, giving me that lazy smile again as her eyes rove my length once more, causing me to shiver. "Let's go," she murmurs, crossing the space between us, cupping my chin in her hands and tilting my face up to meet hers.

She kisses me slowly, lingeringly this time, before she steps back, scooping the towels out of my pack, handing one to me and taking the other and wrapping it tightly around her body. I towel my hair off, running the fabric over my body quickly as I keep stealing little glances at her. She's leaning against the wall next to the door, and she's watching my motions with hooded eyes.

I don't want to let her out of my sights, but I have the feeling that if she *wanted* to leave, there's not a single thing I could do to stop her.

It strikes me, as I toss the towel onto the bench, sneaking a glance at her one more time, that she reminds me of something.

She reminds me of something, well...*wild*.

I rummage around in my pack and take out my clean pair of panties, my other pair of jeans and a dark gray sweater. I slide everything on, leaving my sodden jeans and fleece where they lie on the bench (I hope they're still here tomorrow—I'll bring them back then), and I toss my towel into my pack.

When I turn to look back at her, Shannon is no longer leaning against the wall; instead, she has the door open just a crack, and she's staring out at the darkness surrounding the bathroom with a frown, her chin lifted, her nose to the air.

She's also...sniffing?

"I'm ready to go," I tell her, and she glances back at me, a warm smile spreading over her face as she nods.

"Let's go together," she tells me, and when I nod, ready to walk past her, she reaches out, curling her fingers over my upper arm gently.

"Stay by me," she tells me, her gaze flicking out to the darkness. "If anything happens," she says, working her jaw, "I will keep you safe."

I blink at her, but then I'm shaking my head. "You don't need to keep me safe," I say gently, reaching up and covering her hand on my arm with my own, squeezing. "I can take care of myself," I say, and I mean it. Also, what was she talking about? There's nothing dangerous out in the woods. It's Allegany

State Park. We have rotund, lazy black bears, and that's about it.

She glances at me with surprise, her brows up. "I...I'm sorry," she says, and this suave, smooth woman is actually stammering in front of me. "I didn't mean to offend you," she says, shaking her head. "Of course you can take care of yourself. There are just...dangerous things out in this woods."

"I can take care of myself," I repeat, but my mouth twitches upward at the corners. "But I appreciate the sentiment. That's very sweet."

She smiles at me, too. "I don't doubt that you can," she says, her voice a low growl, but when I walk past her, out into the woods, Shannon lets the bathroom door close behind us, and she remains very, very close by my side, glancing out toward the trees, her nose to the air. Occasionally, I can hear her sniffling, and I glance back, but she's not sniffling. She's actually *sniffing*.

Is she a hunter? A tracker? Does she smell a camper roasting some delicious hot dogs somewhere close by? She catches me watching her, and in the darkness, as we leave the haloed outside light of the bathroom building, I see her white teeth flashing in the dark as she smiles.

But she doesn't offer an explanation.

When we reach my cabin, I unlock my car and drag out my suitcase, locking the trunk behind me. Shannon waits for me up on the porch, glancing out into the woods, her arms crossed in front of her over the towel, her chin lifted, her eyes narrowed. She's beautiful, hauntingly so, as a cool wind moves between the trees, caressing her already drying hair and blowing it to the side, over her shoulder. But she also looks vigilant. Like she's waiting for something to happen. Or perhaps she's waiting for some*one*.

I lug the suitcase up to the porch, and I use my flashlight to help me find the key on my key ring for the cabin. When I turn the lock and open the cabin door, a million memories slam into me, because there is that familiar musty smell, the "you're about to start your vacation" scent of a cabin that hasn't been used for awhile. That scent fills me with memories and anticipations, of all the adventures I've had here, and all the adventures I'm going to have. I spent so much of my life here, and it's so comforting, that smell of old pine and firewood, the ghosts of fires in the potbelly stove in the corner.

I flick the lights on, and the soft glow of the bulbs filters over the wooden walls and cots, the ancient refrigerator unplugged in the corner, and the sagging, equally ancient couch on the far wall. I turn back, pushing the door open, and let Shannon walk past me into the cabin. Then I shut the door behind the both of us, turning the locks.

"You must be cold," Shannon tells me, glancing at me with her brow furrowed. I breathe out into the air, my breath billowing like a cloud of fog between us. Then I nod, shivering a little. I cross the room to the stove, propping it open as I crouch down.

"Aren't you cold?" I ask her, glancing over my shoulder as I begin to crumple old newspaper and shove the wads into the stove's mouth.

She shakes her head, crossing her arms in front of her, her feet hip-width apart. "I don't get cold," she says softly, and I can tell that she's glancing at my rear as I crouch down; a small smile plays at the corners of her mouth.

"Well, while I get this fire going," I tell her, feeling my cheeks flush as I regard her with a smile, "why don't you dig through my suitcase, see if there's something in there that you think will fit you."

She nods, lifting my suitcase up from the floor like it weighs nothing, and she sets it down on the cot closest to her. The cot sags beneath the weight of the suitcase. I...really don't pack light.

Shannon zips the bag open, and I go back to wadding up crumpled newspaper until I'm satisfied with the nest of it that I've put in the stove. I slide in a few small pieces of kindling, and I strike a long match against the box, delighting in the warm glow as I place the tiny flame against the newspaper in the stove. It immediately alights, and I blow out the match, feeding more kindling to the little fire.

I can hear Shannon rummaging around in the suitcase, but the crackling fire absorbs my attention, until I'm absolutely certain that it's not going to go out. Then I stand up, brushing off my knees as I close the stove door. I turn around.

"Um..." I murmur, licking my lips. "Wow."

Shannon has swept her hair up into a messy bun using one of my hair ties, and she's wearing a bit of the jewelry I brought (Yes, I brought jewelry for camping. No, it wasn't intentional. I hadn't unpacked my small jewelry case from my last work trip two weeks ago, and I still had it packed away in the zippered top of my suitcase). She's wearing a black choker, dripping with little black gems, some bracelets and black earrings that twinkle in the soft lights from overhead. She's also wearing a gray tank top that shows off her muscled (and tanned, I realize now) shoulders clearly. The super sexy effect *should* stop there, because she's also wearing my black fleece pajama bottoms that are covered in small orange jack-o-lanterns... And, somehow, they look sexy on her.

"Wow," I repeat, licking my lips again and crossing the space between us. "You look..."

She glances down at the pajama bottoms and laughs. It's the first laugh I've heard her make, and I feel myself breathing out, relaxing, as I listen to that gorgeous sound, that warm, low peal of laughter.

"Ridiculous?" she asks me, one brow up, her hands on her hips as she flicks her gaze to me. "I hope you don't mind," she says, lifting up her arms, the bracelets clacking, "but I wanted to get dolled up. This moment is...special," she says, tilting her head.

And then she turns around and lifts the bottle of red wine out of the suitcase with a teasing smile, swinging it from her fingers, a questioning brow raised.

I brought beer, because of *course* you bring beer camping. But I love wine, and I'd picked up this bottle of red last year and never had a chance to drink it. I thought this trip would be as good a time as any. It's sad that I considered a camping trip the highlight of my year, the time to bring out the good vintage...but there it is.

"I only brought one glass," I tell her apologetically, fishing around in the suitcase for the glass I packed, nestled it in one of my hoodies so that there was no possibility of it getting broken.

"I can drink out of the bottle," she tells me softly, but I shake my head, adamant.

"What, are we animals?" I tell her, shaking my head again, flashing her a small smile. "Nonsense. We can share the glass." I hold it up.

Her mouth twitches at the corners again, but

she nods as I bring the corkscrew up and out of the depths of the suitcase; then I open the bottle of wine.

"I'm not a wine snob or anything," I tell her, as I pour the red liquid into the glass, "which is why I'm not letting it breathe."

She's grinning as I hand her the glass. "I don't believe in waiting," she says, and when I glance at her, surprised at the tone in her voice, her eyes are dark as she watches at me.

"I...do," I tell her with a gulp, but then I take a deep breath and grin at her. "I'm not usually a fast mover," I murmur, setting the open bottle down on the little table next to the bed.

Her smile is pure sex as her eyes rake me over, up and down, and then she cocks her head. She brings the glass of wine up to her nose. "Smells great," she says, swirling the contents gently with her wrist as she turns away from me, moving slowly, her hips swaying.

Shannon sinks down on the ancient coach in the corner then, crossing her legs elegantly and putting her arm up along the back of the couch as she gazes at me, one brow raised in question. "Won't you join me, Abby?" she says, the words a soft, sensual growl as she swirls her glass again, watching me.

I'm trying my best not to overthink this, but as I cross the space between us, as I sit down on the creaking couch beside her, my back poker stiff, I wonder what's happening to me.

Because as I looked at her across the room, my heart skipped a beat. A flush of color sprang up in my cheeks. Desire roared through me.

But there was something more, something beyond all that physical stuff.

There was an ache in my heart as I looked at

her. A good ache. The kind of ache you feel when something broken is on the mend.

Shannon brings the glass up to her lips and closes her eyes. I watch her as she tilts her head back just a little, her full lips closing over the rim of the glass. She takes the tiniest of sips and savors the wine in her mouth for a moment before swallowing. Then she opens those sparkling golden eyes and holds the glass out to me, giving me her small, secret smile.

"Savor it," she whispers, her fingers brushing against mine as I reach out and touch her hand and grasp the glass.

Savor it. I don't think she's talking about the wine.

"I...will," I say softly. She removes her hand, uncrosses her legs slowly, calculatingly...sexily. And then she recrosses them, all the while gazing into my eyes.

I take a sip of the wine, and I'm pleased with how it tastes. Mellow and smoky, with a hint of vanilla and blackberry. Very nice, very subtle. I reach out, setting the glass down on the little, broken wood coffee table that has served this cabin as long as I've been alive (Mom said she garbage-picked it back in the sixties).

And then I turn and look at Shannon.

And I don't say anything. She said to savor this. So that's exactly what I do as I lean forward, the crouch creaking (very unsexily, I might add) beneath me. I lean close to her, and I linger, my face an inch or so from her own.

I can smell the wine on her breath, can smell the pine in her hair as she smiles at me, as she wraps her arms around me, bringing me close. She brushes her hot mouth against my own, and then she kisses me with a fervor that you'd think all of our antics in the shower would have wiped out—but no. She's even more passionate, if that's possible, when she kisses me now, her tongue moving, insistent, her teeth nibbling my lower lip, everything as slow and lovely as a dance. And when she traces kisses across my cheek, down my chin, down my neck, I gasp out against her. She teases me with her tongue and teeth, sucking the skin a little. I think she just gave me a hickey.

"You don't know," she murmurs against me, drawing me even closer to her, "how long I've waited for this, for you..."

And that's when there comes a knock at the door.

Beside me, Shannon lets out a long, low sigh, her entire body stiffening as she stops kissing me, sitting upright, her mouth wet. She turns, glancing at the front door. "No," she murmurs, and when she glances back at me, her eyes are so pain-filled that my heart aches instantaneously, just to see her like that.

"What's wrong?" I whisper, reaching out to touch her, but she's shaking her head, sitting straighter on the couch.

"It's...too late," she murmurs, running her hand through her hair. Then she looks at me, really looks at me, uncrossing her legs, leaning forward, placing a gentle, warm hand on either side of my face, holding me. "Abby," she says then, her golden gaze boring into mine, her tone fast, soft, urgent. "No matter *what* she says to you, you have to believe me, okay? You have to—"

"Abby?" comes a woman's voice, loud and menacing, from the other side of the door. "Are you in there with someone? You might be in danger. Open this door immediately."

The flat way she's speaking, the loud, almost yelling tone, the brusqueness...

It's Barbara at the door, I realize, paling.

I hold Shannon's gaze, but then I break away, standing, crossing the room quickly. For a long moment, my hand hovers over the doorknob, but then I take a deep breath, and I unlock the door. I open it just an inch, peering out into the night.

Barbara.

"Hi," I tell her shortly. "What's going on?"

She's standing on the porch with a flashlight, and she shines it into my eyes. I couldn't see if she had anything else on her person—there are rumors that the park rangers possess guns for bear control, and I thought I saw her holding a shotgun in her hand—but I can't see anything now that I'm blinded from the flashlight.

"Abby, are you in there with someone?" she asks, and she's trying to make her voice sound comforting, I can tell, but it's just really coming across as sickly sweet, cloying, and absolutely, one hundred percent fake.

"What's it to you, Barbara?" I ask her carefully, trying to keep my voice light, but it really doesn't come out sounding like that. The flashlight beam goes out of my eyes, and she sighs for a long moment.

"Abby, it's for your own good if you tell me if you're in there with a strange woman. You would have found her naked, possibly wounded, curly brown hair, tall, lanky. She's on the run, and she's dangerous."

For a very long moment, I'm completely unsure of what to do. But then I startle, because there's a warm, gentle hand on my shoulder.

"She already knows I'm here, Abby," says Shannon, her voice low. "It's all right."

I step back, opening the door a little, and across the threshold, tension crackles as Barbara and Shannon stare at one another. Shannon's shoulders are rolled back, and she has her arms crossed in front of her. Barbara just looks shocked to see her.

"How could you have healed it that quickly?" she mutters, narrowing her eyes in suspicion as she stares at Shannon's bare, healthy shoulder.

"What...what's going on here?" I ask, my voice high because I'm honestly a little scared right now—I have no idea what's going on—but I soldier through that flicker of fear, anyway. "Barbara, what's this all about?" I ask her, my voice sharp now, cutting as I ball my hands into fists. "What makes you think you have any right to—"

But Barbara shakes her head, cutting me off as she steps forward, placing her hand aggressively around Shannon's forearm. "You're coming with *me*," she snarls, "and we're going to finish what we started."

"No," says Shannon tiredly as she looks at Barbara, her lips up and over her teeth. "You're going to cheat and get everything you want. Because you are a coward," she murmurs, almost as an afterthought, but I can see how hard Barbara is gripping Shannon's forearm. Barbara twists it sharply at that moment, but Shannon makes absolutely no sound, still staring at Barbara with hate in her eyes.

"Hey, you can't just barge in here," I start, and I move toward Barbara, but in that moment, she turns her angry stare on me.

And I stop in my tracks.

Her eyes...they honestly look like she's fevered.

Like she's not, in this moment, in her right mind.

She's terrifying.

"No matter what happens, Abby, you have to stay in the cabin," Shannon tells me softly, her words pleading. "Please don't come out. I want you to be safe. You have to stay safe."

And then Barbara moves backward, her fingernails still gripping Shannon's arm, and Shannon follows her out onto the porch, pulling the door shut behind her.

I don't even think, and just as instantly, my hand is on the doorknob, and I'm opening it, rushing out onto the porch, glancing around wildly, looking for the two women.

But Barbara and Shannon are nowhere to be seen.

"What..." I whisper, glancing down.

There are two piles of clothes on the porch. One is a park ranger uniform, with a hat and unlit flashlight resting next to it. The other pile consists of jack-o-lantern PJ bottoms, a gray tank top and my jewelry.

I gasp, crouching down, picking up one of the bangle bracelets and staring at it, still warm from lying against Shannon's skin. I'm half-disbelieving, half-not-really-wanting-to-believe what I'm seeing with my own two eyes. How is this *possible*? One moment I was on the other side of the door, and the next I was out here. There is no way that they could have slipped out of their clothes and disappeared so quickly, and here might be the most pressing question:

Why in the world *would they want to take their clothes off, in the first place?*

Feeling the hair on the back of my neck stand

up, I scoop Barbara's flashlight from the porch floor and flick it on, shining it into the woods on either side of the porch. There's nothing but pine trees and fallen branches and a carpet of leaves, stretching out into the scary-looking woods.

There's nothing, no one, at all.

For a long, cold moment, I stand there, gripping the flashlight, listening to myself breathing, listening to the absurd quiet of the woods that swallowed two full-grown women whole. There is absolutely nothing moving out among the trees, and not a single sound. It's like they just vanished.

But I grip the flashlight, listen as hard as I can to the quiet of the woods around me, and that's when I hear it, out in the forest to my right...

A...growl. A deep, low, savage growl that reverberates through the trees.

My body reacts instantly. I leap off of the porch, and with the flashlight beam bouncing off the tree trunks, I'm dashing into the woods, following the sound.

Running in the woods at night is no small feat, and really, *really* not a fun thing. Small branches keep slapping my face with bright pain, even though I duck beneath as many as I can, and they get tangled in my hair mercilessly. There are branches strewn all over the forest floor, and I leap over as many as I can, but one that I don't see trips me up, and I go crashing to the earth, my hands softening my fall (and delivering some pretty nasty brush-burns to my palms).

The flashlight is knocked wildly out of my hand and is lying now, still lit, next to the trunk of a big oak, the beam illuminating some weeds that move to and fro in the light. A small, chill wind is blowing through the woods now.

I groan a little, rubbing at my palms, and I sit very still for a long moment, listening. But the woods are quiet again. I hear the soft *shush* of the wind in the tree branches around me, causing the hair at the back of my neck to stand on end. I rise gingerly, picking up the flashlight, and I stand motionless, trying to choose a direction. When I turn my flashlight beam toward the forest clearing ahead of me...

I stop, the breath knocked out of my lungs.

Because something impossible is happening in the center of that clearing.

There are two wolves there, and they are fighting each other viciously. It takes me a moment to make sense of that fact, trying to hold my flashlight as steadily as I can in my hand, because I realize, right now, I'm shaking. The two wolves in the clearing are rolling end over end, snarling and growling and biting and snapping. My flashlight beam catches them as they perform a particularly epic flip, one wolf getting shoved out of the clearing, its paws skidding in the earth as it rights itself very close to me.

This wolf has dark brown fur, mottled in black.

It looks...familiar.

I stare at it for a long moment, my eyes going wider as I realize that this is the wolf I thought I saw in the bathroom. But how is that possible?

How is *this* possible?

I don't get time to think about it or even to react to the fact that a wolf just came so close to me. The wolf gets up, rising quickly to its four paws, and shakes itself off, its ruff bouncing to and fro. And then it glances in my direction.

I flash the beam of light into its eyes, and for a

long moment, we remain frozen in place, the wolf looking into the light, and me staring back, eyes narrowed. And then I sit down quickly on the ground, the strength leaving my legs as I crumple, as I gaze into the golden eyes set in that wolf's face.

I'm not staring into wolf eyes.

I'm looking at *human* eyes.

Eyes I've seen before.

Panic roars through me. Because...no. It can't be. *Can't* be...but...

If you asked me what I think I see...

This is so crazy.

But the wolf has *Shannon's* eyes.

It's not possible. I know, absolutely, that this isn't possible.

The wolf shakes itself again, lifting its face to the air, its nose wrinkling, sniffing. I watch it leap back into the center of the meadow, bounding toward the much bigger wolf, with its much bigger teeth, and in that moment, I'm compelled to step closer, to aim my flashlight beam on the two wolves who are standing off from each other, circling one another, hackles up, snarling as they pace.

This other wolf is *huge*. The first wolf, the one that came close to me, stands as tall as my hips. But this other animal? Its shoulders are as tall as *my* shoulders. I feel like a broken record at this point, but I have to reiterate: *how is that even possible?* The wolf is a typical gray color, but everything about it is a little off, a little wrong: its rippling muscles, its massive height and very large, pointy teeth make it much more imposing than the smaller wolf. And it seems to know this, as it snarls fearlessly, lunging for the smaller wolf.

I shouldn't be here, watching this. I should be

running away as fast as I can, back toward the cabin. I should be trying to find Barbara and Shannon.

But that wolf's eyes...

Okay. It's been a very strange night. I could have never predicted or expected any of this. And I know this sounds crazy, and I couldn't tell you exactly why...but I'm utterly compelled to watch this fight...

Well. That's not exactly true.

I'm utterly compelled to root for the smaller wolf.

At first, I try to explain it away: people always root for the underdog (or, you know, under*wolf*, as the case may be). But the plain, cold truth is that I shouldn't be rooting for *either* of them. I should be terrified, running away in abject fear.

But for some weird reason...I'm not.

Oh, don't get me wrong: I'm afraid of that big wolf, the way the ground seems to shake when its paws touch down as it paces, hackles up, circling the smaller wolf. But I'm not terrified enough to get myself away to safety. And, honestly, it's not as if either of the wolves are really paying attention to me; they're too absorbed in each other. The first one, the smaller one, did glance in my direction, but she hasn't looked my way since...

Huh. I'm thinking of her as a *she* now.

That's...weird.

I watch the two wolves lunge at each other, and I try to make peace with how big the one wolf is. Maybe it's just a skewed perspective. The larger gray wolf can't possibly be *that* large. Maybe there was something in the wine, something that causes strong hallucinations. I know that I'm not dreaming, but I *also* know that a wolf is never as tall as a horse.

As I aim my flashlight beam at the wolves circling each other, low growling filling the clearing, I gulp. My light isn't strong, but it's strong enough to see that the smaller wolf's back is slick with blood, and that her right leg is cut severely; I'm assuming the wound was inflicted by the other wolf's teeth.

And there isn't a mark on the other wolf, not a piece of fur out of place.

As it circles the smaller wolf, the smaller wolf who lifts up her paw, limping, trying to keep the bigger wolf in front of her at all times...it almost looks as if the bigger one is...smiling.

I shiver, training the flashlight beam back on the smaller wolf.

But that's when the bigger one turns, its nose in the air, its ears pricked forward.

Oh, God...

It's looking at me.

It finally noticed me.

Fear, cold and sharp, rises in me instantly as it turns toward me, its lip curling up higher over its extremely long, extremely white teeth. It lowers its head, and I know, unmistakably, that this is what it looks like when it's hunting something.

The big wolf begins to pad slowly toward me.

Oh, my God. I'm shaking so hard that I almost drop the flashlight, but I think back on everything my parents ever told me about bears. Bears are like wolves, right? If you make a lot of noise, bears don't want to mess with you and will leave you alone.

If I turn and run, it's going to come after me, I just know it. I know how dogs operate; I know that dogs love to chase running things. Surely a wolf would, too. And if that massive creature comes barreling toward me, I don't stand a chance.

So I grab hold of every last scrap of courage inside of myself, and I take a single step forward.

"Hey... Hey, you!" I shout as loudly as I can, waving my arms and the flashlight beam back and forth, very quickly, in its eyes. The wolf is still in the clearing, but it's rapidly closing the distance between us since its legs are so long.

"Hey, you, get out of here!" I shout, kicking leaves up with my legs, trying to be as loud and scary-to-a-wild-animal as possible. I jump up and down, waving my arms, feeling my heart in my throat as the wolf advances.

Yeah, it's not even flinching at my antics.

That's when I realize that I'm in really, *really* big trouble.

The massive thing advances on me as I hold the flashlight in my shaking hand and try to keep the beam trained on its face. But I have to point the flashlight beam *up*, and when the wolf gets within ten feet of me, I'm having trouble breathing, because...it's true: the wolf really *is* that big. It's as tall as I am, even when it's just standing on all fours.

Impossible. But whether it's impossible or not, it's real, and it's right in front of me.

The wolf stomps its front right paw down, its lips over teeth as long as my fingers. It snarls at me, then, its lip wrinkling as the low growl causes my entire body to vibrate. And it does almost look like it's smiling as it lowers its head, as it lowers its whole body, its eyes unblinking and trained on me.

It's getting ready to spring on me, I realize. To spring on me and sink its enormous teeth into my skin and eat me up.

I brace myself. And I take a deep breath, tensing.

But the wolf doesn't attack me. Because the smaller wolf chooses that moment to ram itself into the side of the big gray wolf. The big wolf hardly moves when the smaller animal collides with it, but it moves quickly, turning, snarling, picking up the smaller wolf in its teeth and shaking her like a rag doll.

I gasp, my hand over my mouth as the smaller wolf goes sailing into a tree, thrown by the big wolf's jaws. And I couldn't tell you why I do it; my body moves of its own accord: I run straight toward the fallen wolf.

I kneel down beside it, tears springing into my eyes as I see all of the lacerations and wounds crisscrossing the creature's body. It's obvious that the larger wolf has every advantage, and still this wolf bravely fought it. Why? None of this makes sense. Just like it makes no sense that I was compelled to see if the wolf was all right. I can't help it. I can't save it. And it's a wild animal—I shouldn't even be trying.

But that's when the wolf looks up at me again, her golden eyes glowing. Those beautiful, golden eyes that are so incredibly familiar. I gulp down air; a tear courses over my cheek.

It's crazy, ludicrous, what I'm about to do, but I do it, anyway.

"Shannon?" I whisper into the dark.

And slowly, painfully, the wolf blinks her golden eyes—and she nods her head.

I breathe out, my heart rate skyrocketing as the wolf rolls over, as she gingerly climbs to her feet, limping as she holds up her front right paw. She gazes back at the big wolf, and she lifts her chin proudly.

Is this even happening? I feel the muddy ground beneath my knees, feel the flashlight in my hands. It all feels very real, too real. I draw in a deep breath as the smaller wolf lunges, again, for the bigger one.

Did she really nod?

Is she really Shannon?

I try to piece everything together in my head as I pale further. Earlier tonight, there was a wolf—this wolf—in the center of the bathroom floor, and when I looked again, a few *seconds* later, Shannon was there. At the time, it was convenient to think that I'd imagined the wolf (but, really, is this something people *imagine*? I mean, my imagination is pretty good, but not *that* good!). But now, thinking about it...

My mouth goes dry.

Do I really believe that the wolf in front of me is Shannon? And that she's, well, a werewolf? That's utterly insane.

But I entertain the thought for a nanosecond. Because if that wolf is Shannon, does that mean that this other wolf...

Is *Barbara*?

I think back on all the times Barbara made me feel uneasy when I was growing up, all the things about her that never quite made sense. I was, instinctively, scared of her, even though I wasn't usually scared of adults, not even the adults I *should* have been scared of. There was just something ominous about her that I felt but never could place, and sometimes, when she looked at me...

I try to breathe, find that I'm kind of failing.

Barbara always looked like she wanted to eat me.

The larger wolf chooses this exact moment to look back over its shoulder. It just bit the smaller wolf again, delivering a vicious wound to her back left leg. Blood leaks down onto the carpet of leaves at the wolves' feet. The bigger wolf staring back at me now licks its lips, and it turns, coming for me.

Oh, my God. I scramble to my feet, keeping the flashlight beam trained on the wolf. I peer over its shoulder, and my heart sinks as I catch sight of the smaller wolf, trying to stand, swaying.

Whatever is happening right now, whether it's two wolves fighting, or whether it's two werewolves fighting...the big one is winning.

And the smaller one doesn't stand a chance.

I feel, in my gut, that this isn't right. There's something in me that deems this as incredibly unfair.

I'm not an extraordinarily brave person, but justice is pretty important to me. It also helps, adrenaline-wise, that I'm about to get eaten by this big wolf. I take two steps forward and swing my flashlight—the big, heavy-duty park ranger flashlight that Barbara had been carrying—at the wolf's head.

The metal flashlight connects with bone, and there is a sickening *thud*. The wolf yelps, taking a step back, sneezing and shaking its head.

And that's when the smaller wolf steps up.

And she lunges at the big wolf.

Again, they go rolling end over end, but this time, it's the smaller wolf who comes out on top, snarling as she clamps her jaws around the bigger wolf's throat, a lucky gamble, but she's clinging to its throat, biting down for all she's worth.

For a long moment, nothing happens. The two wolves stand there, the smaller one gripping the bigger wolf's throat in her jaws. But then, with a shuddering groan, the bigger wolf rolls down, lying on its side on the ground, crumpling.

And before my eyes, something very strange happens.

The big gray wolf begins to shrink. That's the best way to describe what I'm seeing, what I'm *impossibly* seeing, but there it is: the wolf is growing smaller. But that's not all that's happening. The wolf's back legs grow longer, while its front legs grow shorter, and its nose begins to push back, into its head...

At the same time that the fur begins to disappear...

I stare as a woman's shape begins to materialize out of the mass of wolf. A woman's shape that becomes, in a few short heartbeats...Barbara.

At the same time, the smaller wolf is changing, too, though her outline blurs much quicker. One moment, I think I'm staring at a wolf, and the next moment I'm not.

Because there—on the forest floor—is Barbara, kneeling down, growling, completely naked. While Shannon stands beside her, swaying on her two feet, blood dripping down her arms...also completely naked.

The two women stare at each other, ice in their eyes, their breath puffing out of their mouths like ghosts.

"Is this..." I whisper, gasping. "Is this...really happening?"

And though my words were very, very quiet, Shannon, ten feet from me, nods resolutely.

"Yes. It's really happening, Abby," she growls softly, glancing up at me quickly, then back down to Barbara, still glaring daggers up at her from her kneeling position. Barbara's hand is at her neck, massaging the back of it almost ruefully.

When Shannon stares down at Barbara, there is anger in face, yes. But there's also pain. Blood is dripping from her wounds onto the leaves at her feet, blood pouring out of several wounds, more than I can see. My heart is in my throat.

"You'll still have to leave," says Barbara then, her voice twisted into a terrible, wolfish snarl as she sneers up at Shannon, spitting on the ground at her feet. "You know that no one saw us fight. This," she says, waving her hand between them, "*doesn't count*. You will *never* catch me off my guard again," she says, her mouth in a wide, leering smile, "and unless the pack saw the fight—it's over. You will *never* be alpha."

"What going on?" I ask weakly, and Shannon glances quickly at me again before staring back down at Barbara, her eyes distant.

For a long moment, no one speaks. Barbara pants, Shannon breathes slowly, carefully, and I watch the two of them in disbelief.

Finally, Shannon's lips part. "I've lived here all my life," she says then, tiredly, in explanation. "Well...around here. In Olean, really. I was part of a pack that Barbara ran. But Barbara," Shannon snarls then, "is not a, shall we say, *good person*. And she took the pack from my mother by force. My mother was a good alpha. But Barbara murdered her," she whispers into the air.

I stare at Barbara, my eyes wide. I remember all of the times I feared that woman. Though all of this is very hard to make sense of, I can make sense of this much: I was right. Barbara is not, as Shannon put it, a good person.

Wolf Pack

"I wanted to get back what was my mother's," says Shannon, lifting her face and glancing at me now. There are bright tears standing in her golden eyes, and it breaks my heart to see them. "And to become an alpha, you must challenge the current alpha. And I did," she whispers. "And I lost, due to a technicality," Shannon spits out bitterly.

"Of course you lost," growls Barbara then. "You're as weak as your mother." She rises smoothly to her feet, with a wide smile.

But Shannon turns. And the look that comes over her face, her golden eyes flashing with such a hateful, intense fire, renders her terrifying. Shannon's entire body tenses, and she takes one long, slow, calculating step closer to Barbara.

"Be *ready*," she whispers, the words carrying into the night.

Those are, apparently, the words spoken when a werewolf fight is on, because Barbara snarls, and as I watch, her human face suddenly loses its humanity, watch her teeth grow long, pointy, terrifying. And I'm *shocked* in that moment how quickly Shannon transforms. She is Shannon, the human I know—the human I made love to not an hour ago—one moment, and within the very next heartbeat, she is something else entirely. She is a wolf, and she throws back her head.

And she *howls*.

It is mournful, like every recording of a wolf I've ever heard, but there is something else to it, in the darkness. Something sad and long and low and beautiful. The music of it makes my heart rise and ache, all at once.

But then Shannon isn't howling anymore.

Instead, she's lowering her head, and she gazes at Barbara, and she lunges for the much bigger wolf-woman. Barbara is only half-transformed, is right now a weird-looking half-human, half-wolf hybrid, with pointy teeth and extra-long ears and patchy fur all over her naked body. The two creatures meet, and they tumble across the forest floor together, snarling and snapping and growling, their claws or half-claws trying to gain purchase on each other's bodies, their teeth scrabbling to make contact and create pain.

As I stare at them, as I train my flashlight beam on them, trying to make out who might be winning this time, I feel a strange presence at my back.

I turn, every hair on the back of my neck standing up, and I see them, so *many* of them:

Wolves.

They flow around me as if I'm a stone in the middle of a river. They move fluidly, in sync, like the pack they are. I count about fifteen wolves before I stop counting, before I take a step back, gulping as they move past me, not even glancing in my direction.

They're staring at the two women, the two wolves, locked in combat, their noses pointed to the pair like a north star. The wolves' pelts range in color from red to somber gray to black, and though they are all very different, these wolves have one thing in common.

They pause in their relentless motion. They stand still, the wind moving across their fur, and as they stand together, they throw back their heads.

They lift their faces to the moon, a slim sickle of light overhead.

And they howl.

The two wolves fighting in the forest clearing—

Wolf Pack

each of them fully formed now—pause in the midst of their battle. They back off from one another, huffing, shaking their ruffs, and they glance back at the other wolves.

And, folding forward, growing fluidly, the fur disappearing into her smooth, tan skin, Shannon transforms to her human self.

I wrap my arms tightly around myself, my hair still standing on end.

What's happening? I want to ask her, as she stares at the other wolves, eyes wide. But I don't say a word. I remain crouched, silent.

Shannon only nods once, and then she turns to me.

"They're speaking," Shannon whispers, and she watches me with tears in her eyes. "They said that they saw me defeat her. They said that it's over. That I'm alpha now." Shannon is shaking her head, stepping forward. "They say," she murmurs, gazing at me with her warm golden eyes, "that because you were here and you saw it...it counts. They felt it and heard it, but you were *here*."

Barbara is also in her human form now, and she's snarling at me. "Of *course* she doesn't count!" she bellows at the other wolves. "She is not part of the pack! She's not even *were!* This is *insane!*"

I turn to glance back at all of the wolves, but they're not looking at me; their noses are up, quivering as they sniff in the dark. And they are all looking at Shannon. So I turn back, and I look at her, too. I look at her shining, golden eyes as she comes close to me, gathering me in her arms and drawing me to her.

"You've been coming here since you were very small," she whispers then, into my ear, her breath warm against my skin, her bare body radiating heat against me. I sigh, lowering my head to her shoulder, all of the adrenaline pooling out of me. "I saw you," she murmurs to me, nuzzling my hair with her nose, kissing my neck. "I saw you back then, when I was a kid, too. You belong here. You've always belonged here. You count."

Barbara snarls, but all of the wolves remain silent and still, sentinels staring at her. I can't tell what they're saying, but this much is clear: it's over. Barbara stands for a long moment, staring at the two of us with such anger and hatred on her face that the poison of it is palpable in the air. But then she's limping past us as the other wolves circle, moving with her, escorting her away, the lot of them disappearing into the woods like so much smoke.

And that leaves just the two of us standing here—one woman fully clothed, and, you know, human. The other completely naked.

And, you know, a *werewolf*.

"This is...this is all so crazy," I whisper to Shannon as she takes my face in her hands, gazing down at me.

"I know," she says, brow wrinkling, her mouth turning up ruefully at the corners. "I'm sorry for that. Most weres never even tell their partners what they are... You know, the whole worldview imploding thing." She chuckles again, and again, the sound of her laughter, so rich and warm, makes a shiver of happiness run through me.

Yeah, it's impossible that this is happening. But it *is* happening.

I'm just going to go with it.

"You know," I tell her, my heart beginning to

beat even faster, "I...um. Well, my family owns this cabin," I tell her with a small smile, gesturing back through the trees in the direction that I think the cabin might be.

Shannon raises a single brow.

"This is the oddest one-night stand ever," I tell her, and I'm smiling a little more now. "But I...really like you. Um. Everything is weird, and it's going to take some getting used to," I say, "but...can I possibly...see you again?"

She's grinning now. Grinning like a wolf.

"I'd like that," she says, leaning down and kissing me. It is a fierce kiss, a soft kiss, and she tastes like pine and mint and cold, fall evenings, like the evening curling around us now, the forest moving quietly, each branch dancing in a soft, chill wind.

"So," I tell her, when we finally break away for air, "if it's not a one-night stand..." I lift my brows, too, as I smile a little at her. "That would make this... A first date?"

She laughs again, pulling me close, an arm around my shoulders as she shakes her head, the warmth of her body radiating into me. "The oddest first date ever."

I smile at her and give her another small kiss, wrapping my arms around her bare waist.

"Oh, I don't know," I tell her, her heat chasing away the cold of the night. "I liked it," I tell her, which is a stretch for some of the activities of the evening...but then I tell her the absolute truth, breathing it out into the cool, dark air, "I like *you*."

She raises a lovely brow, and then she's grinning as she pulls me back toward the cabin. Her wounds, I'm realizing, are already gone. I apparently have a lot to learn about werewolves.

"Let's see if I can get you to *love* this date, then," she tells me, her voice soft and low, sending a shiver of pleasure racing through me.

I take her hand and let her draw me back to the cabin, where the warm glow of light spills out through the familiar, comforting windows, chasing away the dark.

Wolf Pack

-- A Wolf for Valentine's Day --

"Seriously, Trish—no one wants to spend Valentine's Day *alone*!"

I stare at my sister with narrowed eyes as I try very, *very* hard to concentrate on taking deep breaths. I count to ten. I only make it to *four* before Jackie crosses her arms in front of her, puts on her classic big-sister-pout and goes for broke: "we all *know* you're still going to be single on Valentine's Day anyway," she tells me with a shrug. "So, really, why not make the best of it?"

Five, I count carefully in my head, feeling steam pour of my ears. *Six*...

"Jackie," I say then, applauding myself internally for how utterly calm I sound. "It's *Christmas Day*." I gesture around to the mound of torn wrapping paper and ribbon strewn around us, Jackie's kids busily trying to hack into the packaging for a brand new Tonka truck with blunt safety scissors, our mother already passed out on the couch, her glass of sherry beside her on the side table. I shift my weight uncomfortably in my seat, wishing I'd had the foresight to pour *myself* a glass of sherry. "This is really the last day *anyone* should be thinking about Valentine's Day," I mutter with a sigh.

I glance down again at the last present I just unwrapped, peeling off the ribbon and bow from the small envelope with mounting trepidation. "Merry Christmas, Trish!" is scrawled across the top of the envelope in a red, glittery gel pen, in my sister's characteristic uber-neat penmanship.

I had, of course, reason to be dreading what might be inside that innocent-looking envelope. Historically, gifts from my sister that come in envelopes are, shall we say, *unique*.

There was, for example, the time that she thought I'd been "packing on the pounds," (her "trying to be helpful" words, not mine), and she'd signed me up for this crazy Swedish gym downtown where they tried to sweat weight off of you by making you take five-hour long saunas while drinking glass after glass of salt water. "What?" she'd asked me defensively when I opened the envelope, read the gift certificate and my jaw fell open. "It's all the rage in Sweden!" she'd told me.

There was that time that she'd gotten me a gift certificate for a "night with the polar bears" at the local zoo, because—and I quote my sister here—"you're a vet! You *love* animals!" It's true—I do love animals. But what I thought was a fund-raising gala at the zoo was an *actual night with the polar bears*, where a few brave souls were supposed to spend the night in the enclosure with the polar bears to try to set some sort of record for a "man versus bear" television show.

There was also that time my sister gave me a gift certificate to an exotic animal pet store that mostly sold monkeys, because, again, "I love animals."

As you can see, my sister has good intentions.
Sort of.

She's just *really* not good at giving gifts.

So what I have in my hands today is another gift certificate. But this one isn't to a monkey store or for a night with polar bears or for hours and hours of sauna time.

No. Somehow, this one is a little worse.

Because I now hold a gift certificate that reads: "good for three nights at Rainbow Yoga's Annual Valentine's Day Singles Retreat!"

"Oh, Jackie," I tell her with a little grimace. And then, because I'm not sure how to word this properly, I rise, making a beeline for the kitchen and the open bottle of sherry.

"Trish, seriously, I *really* thought you'd be thrilled!" says my sister with a huff, following me through the swinging doors into the kitchen. I can tell she's pissed at me—her long ponytail is tossed over her shoulder, and she's twirling her finger through it like she used to do when I got gum stuck to something she loved when we were younger, or when I read her pink diary when she was in high school. But my sister isn't that person anymore—and I'm no longer the little sister who wreaked havoc on her My Little Pony collection with safety scissors.

We're both grown adults, and we both have very different lives to lead.

Like my sister. Who's soccer mom extraordinaire. She's wearing a velour track suit right now, a headband in her hair, because after we all came to mom's house for Christmas breakfast, Jackie informed us that she's going to go jogging before Christmas brunch because "she has someone to watch the kids." My sister who brought her yoga mat with her to our Christmas day festivities, because she said she needed to squeak in some time for yoga today while she was here.

I'm surprised she didn't bring her mobile scrapbooking unit along with her.

We stare at each other across the kitchen island as I pour two glasses of sherry. I raise an eyebrow and slide one of the glasses across the granite counter top toward Jackie.

"You and I both know you're still going to be single in February," she sniffs, picking up the glass and narrowing her eyes as she glares at me. "I was *just* trying to be helpful."

I take a very deep breath.

"Helpful," I repeat, downing the glass of sherry in one burning gulp. "Jackie..." I say, taking another deep breath and setting the glass down on the counter. I shake my head, not entirely certain how to phrase what—to me, at least—is painfully obvious. I settle on: "while I very much appreciate the gesture, it's not exactly helpful that you want to help your 'pathetic' sister get a girl because you don't think I'm capable of that myself." I wrap my fingers tightly around the stem of the sherry glass and raise an eyebrow.

"I would never say *pathetic*," Jackie tells me with a shake of her head, her ponytail flopping over her shoulder again as she twirls it around her finger, her frown deepening. "It's definitely a little *sad*," she tells me innocently, "but not *pathetic*."

"How is it your place to try to fix this? As if I even *want* it to be fixed?" I tell her, tapping my fingernails on the counter. "I *like* being single," I tell her then fiercely, holding up my hand when she starts to argue. "Do you even *know* how many hours I put in every week at my job? Being a veterinarian isn't some nice little sit-com where I sit around and pet puppies and kitties all day," I tell her, feeling my words sharpen. "I don't have *time* for—"

"Like you're going any younger?" my sister

snaps at me. "Trish, you're thirty-five! When was the last time you were on a date?"

"When was the last time it was *any* of your concern?" I ask her, folding my arms in front of me obstinately.

"It isn't!" she admits, which actually surprises me. Jackie seems subdued for a solid five seconds before she rallies, leaning forward, blustering at me: "But *whatever* about the fact that it's a singles retreat! God knows the yoga will do you good!"

At that I actually chuckle. "Jackie," I tell her, softening as I come around the counter. I take my sister by the shoulders and give her a tiny, good natured shake. "I am the *last* person in the *world* who's ever wanted to try yoga." I let her go, running a hand through my short brown hair. I shrug a little, lean back on the counter. "Where is this place, anyway...this *Rainbow Yoga* center?" I lift my brow as I say the name and try not to smile.

"It's in Boulder, Colorado," my sister tells me smugly, leaning back on the counter, too. When I glance at her with raised eyebrows, she shrugs. "I had David pay for it before we got our divorce back in October," she tells me, her head to the side, her eyes flashing with the familiar impishness that my sister has always been practically famous for.

I snort at that. "Really? You had your ex-husband pay for my Christmas present?" I consider the envelope, lifting up the sherry glass again, ready for another refill.

"Yeah, well, we all know what was happening with him and his secretary, and I wanted a little payback for all that," she tells me with another shrug, leaning into her elbows on the counter.

For a long moment, neither of us says anything as we both stare down at the envelope.

"Boulder, Colorado," I tell her again, voice soft and wistful as I stare out the kitchen window at the sturdy palm tree in the backyard, waving its palm fronds in the warm Christmas day breeze. "Boulder, Colorado," I repeat, "in *February*."

"I know how much you love snow. That's one thing I *do* know," Jackie tells me with a small smile, bumping her shoulder gently against mine. "I'm sorry—I didn't mean to imply you were pathetic. Honest," she says then, biting her lip. "I really *was* trying to be helpful. I can't ever tell if you're telling the truth when you tell me that you're too busy for a girlfriend, or if you're...really not that busy, but you're just not getting out there. You're not a big sister," she tells me, shaking her head. "It's my job to worry about these kinds of things."

I sigh, filling up our glasses again. "I'm not lying to you," I promise her. "I really *am* too busy for any kind of relationship commitment right now."

But even as the words come out of my mouth, I can feel the lie sour.

It's true—I'm definitely busy.

But it's not the *whole* truth.

I open the envelope again, stare down at the gift certificate, taking out the brochure for the place. Rainbow Yoga. It's probably full of hippie women and tie dye and people talking about feelings all the time...which isn't bad. It's just not my scene. I'm the science lady. I sigh a little, take a deep breath, open the brochure.

"The gift certificate comes with free massages, three organic meals a day—I mean, it's *nice*, sis," Jackie promises me, peering at the brochure over my shoulder. "I mean, you could go to the retreat and not even do a bit of yoga if you didn't want to." I can hear the familiar wheedling tone in her voice, the type of tone she's notorious for using when she's trying to manipulate someone into doing something.

"It's not that I'm not grateful for this," I tell her with a big sigh. "And I'm pretty pleased that you had that asshole pay for it," I tell her with a wink as I slide the brochure back into the envelope. "And I love you," I tell her, leaning over and squeezing my sister tightly around the shoulders. "But yoga...a singles retreat...even the very word *retreat*." I run my fingers through my hair again nervously, shake my head. "I mean, it's all moot. I probably couldn't get the time off from my practice, honestly—we've been swamped with new clients. And the thought was very nice," I tell her again, smiling half-heartedly, "but it's just not...really my scene."

Jackie taps the envelope with a finger and slides it across the space between us on the counter to rest beside my elbow. "Just do me a favor and think about it, okay?" she tells me with a small smile. "After all, like you said—it's a long way to Valentine's Day. You have time to think about it. No need to make any decisions right this very minute."

We toast each other with the sherry and drink it down, while Bing Crosby sings about White Christmases on one of the balmiest Christmas days West Palm Beach, Florida, has ever seen.

She's right. Valentine's Day is a long ways off. And it was *really* nice of Jackie to do this for me. But now's not the time to think about it. Valentine's Day is almost two months away. I don't have to decide now.

So I put it out of my mind.

"Miss Dalton," says Elizabeth, knocking loudly on my office door. "Can I have a moment?" she asks me, her brows up.

I glance up from the myriad spreadsheets I'm trying to make sense of on my laptop. My eyes are practically crossed, and when I look up at my secretary, standing in my office doorway, all I really see is blurred numbers instead of her warm, kind face.

"What's up, Elizabeth?" I ask her, rubbing at my eyes and leaning back in my desk chair. Elizabeth flicks on the overhead light in my office, and I wince down in the chair, not a little unlike a vampire exposed to too much sunlight.

"You've been at it for hours," Elizabeth tells me gently, taking in the papers strewn across the desk, the multiple cups of cold coffee sitting by my elbow and my hunched back. I try to lean back a little against the chair, but wince again—God, my back is killing me. "It's Sunday evening, Miss Dalton," says Elizabeth with a sigh. "Aren't you hungry? Don't you want a break?"

My secretary is in her fifties, is full of vinegar when I need her to be, and sugar the rest of the time. But right now, I can tell that there's more than an ounce of vinegar in her tone. She only ever calls me "Miss Dalton" when she's being firm. "No, Elizabeth, I'm fine—really," I promise her with a long sigh, opening the top drawer of my desk to rifle through the takeout menus for another quick dinner option. "I have to go through all of this billing's cycle, and—"

"What you *really* need to do is to hire an assistant," says Elizabeth, shaking her head and placing her hands on her hips in her patented no-nonsense manner. "I'm serious. You're the veterinarian. It's your job to take care of the patients, not their many, many charts. An assistant can do that for you, and you'll get some hours of your life back. It's a win-win," she tells me, raising a single brow.

"I keep meaning to hire one," I tell her, which—even to my ears—sounds like a very lame excuse.

"Well, good, because I already put an ad in the paper about it," says Elizabeth, her head to the side as she smiles widely at me.

I drop the stack of takeout menus back in the drawer and sigh. "Is this a hostile takeover?" I ask her with a wink. Elizabeth shakes her head, and then she sets something down in front of me on my desk.

Suddenly, I don't feel so hungry anymore.

"Your sister called," says Elizabeth blandly, tapping the envelope still marked with "Merry Christmas!"

"And?" I ask her, not touching the envelope.

"She asked me to come into your office and set this down in front of you and, I quote her directly here, 'give you a meaningful look.'" Elizabeth stares down at me with one brow raised over the edge of her glasses, her arms folded in front of her. "So, I've given you the meaningful look. And I've called ahead for the plane tickets and to make sure your room was still reserved at the, ah, Rainbow Yoga place," she tells me, her eyes twinkling.

"I really can't go," I splutter. "You know my

hands are tied. I have appointments all next week," I tell her, gesturing to my calendar, heavily marked with sharpie and actually stapled to my office wall.

"Lucky for you, I cleared them all. And, anyway, Margaret wanted more clients," says Elizabeth, naming the veterinarian I just hired. "There's no reason in the world you shouldn't go to this," she tells me. "It'll be *nice*!"

"I have a reason for you," I tell Elizabeth, shaking my head. "And it's really the most obvious one." I hold up a single finger. "I *don't like yoga*! I mean, I've never done it in my entire life!" I shrug a little, flustered. "Honestly, I don't know the first *thing* about yoga! Who the hell doesn't know a single *thing* about yoga and goes to a yoga *retreat*?"

Elizabeth shrugs. "There's a first time for everything, right? Your plane leaves tomorrow. If you'll go," she tells me, rocking back on her heels, her head to the side as she considers me. "On a nice vacation," she says, enunciating each word, her eyes narrowing, "that's been already paid for..." She trails off.

Elizabeth has been my assistant for as long as I've been a vet. She knows me backwards and forwards and knows exactly how hard to push, and exactly when to let me make my own decisions.

I stare down at the envelope. Admittedly, it would be *utterly stupid* not to go—I know that. My sister had her ex-husband pay for this, she really was thinking of my best interests, and there's absolutely no law that says that, once I get there, I have to do a single *second* of yoga. I could spend the entire time getting massages, ordering in room service, taking in the beautiful snow and city...

It'd be stupid not to go.

I sigh, running a hand through my hair as I prop my elbows up on my desk and grin at my secretary.

It's been a *really* long time since I took a vacation, after all...

"Okay. Could you please send my sister a thank you card? I guess I'll be seeing you next week," I tell Elizabeth, and she casts me a knowing smirk and makes her way out of my office.

Wow. An actual vacation. I stare at the pile of papers on my desk and lean back in my chair, feeling overwhelmed by the very thought.

But everything will still be here when I get back, I remind myself.

That night I get home and pack my cold weather gear, surprised by how excited about this I'm actually becoming. Now that I've convinced myself that I don't have to do a single minute's worth of yoga there—or spend any time with the other "singles" who will be at the retreat—I'm actually excited about the prospect of a vacation.

Unfortunately, I don't actually have a lot of cold weather gear—it's been a long time since I took a vacation to someplace in the winter. Usually people come to Florida for winter—people don't generally leave the balmy breezes and beaches of Florida when the rest of the country is a frozen ice box.

So now that I've promised myself that I'm not going to do yoga—it's really, *really* just not my thing—I'm wondering what sort of skiing options are around Boulder. I've never gone skiing, but it seems like it'd be my speed. I drag my parka down from the attic and dig my snow boots out from under my bed (a really rotten place to keep them, actually, since my cat Reggie likes to stuff his millions of toy mice into them). I pack my suitcase, and I leave it by the door. I call my cat sitter and then go out and buy a case of Reggie's favorite wet food so that he's not *too* angry at me for leaving. I cuddle with him on the couch, smoothing his fluffy black fur while he purrs in my arms, and I promise him that it's just a short trip, and I'll be back very soon. This won't exactly help my case when I don't show up tomorrow and he gets Very Angry, but then Reggie forgives me after every trip. Usually.

I have everything set out, everything prepared, and I fall into my bed utterly exhausted.

And, the next morning, I promptly sleep through my alarm.

I honestly haven't taken a vacation in...well. Let's see. Okay, so I can't actually *remember* the last time I took a vacation, which goes to show you that I really am in need of one. I'm so tired from all of the constant work that piles up at our little clinic that the very first moment of vacation—this morning—I sleep right past the annoying buzzer of my alarm, blaring about six inches away from my head.

My sister was right. I really *do* need a vacation.

I finally get up, my ears ringing with the alarm sounds, exactly an hour and a half before my plane is supposed to take off. In a pure and total panic, I leap out of bed, into my jeans and t-shirt and light jacket I'd laid out the night before, and after kissing Reggie's furry little head, I'm sprinting out of the house with one shoe on and one shoe off, hopping on one foot as I try to put the other shoe on, dragging my suitcase behind me.

I speed pretty badly on the way to the airport, but thankfully there doesn't seem to be many cops out today. I get through security, running like the Devil himself is on my heels as I bolt toward my gate.

And I'm the last person through.

"You're lucky," the flight attendant tells me, holding the door for me so that I can trot down the ramp and into the airplane. The flight attendant is a pretty thing, tall and blonde, with a sideways smile on as she actually winks at me.

That smile and wink are the most action I've gotten in...again...well... Let's just say a very long time. As I pull my suitcase behind me, I feel a smile come over my face, like sunshine spilling out from behind a bank of clouds.

I'm not the type to believe in luck or good omens, or, really, anything like that. But a pretty blonde flight attendant winking at me has got to be a good sign, right? I'd be stupid to ignore that, just like I would have been stupid, I realize, not to come on this trip.

Once I sit down in the airplane and buckle myself in, I take out the brochure from my purse where I packed it, the one for the Rainbow Yoga place. It's a nice brochure, cleanly designed—surprisingly, it doesn't give off a very new age-y vibe, which I would have assumed from the name of the place. I wonder, in the back of my head, if maybe (just maybe) my assumptions about this place are wrong.

I definitely have a bad habit of assuming things about places and people, but...come on. *Rainbow Yoga?* The very name conjures a place in my head full of sprouts and hemp and...that sort of stuff. And not that there's *anything* wrong with that...

I put on my headphones, listen to my favorite classical music mix as the plane takes off. I know that

Wolf Pack

I'm stuck in my ways and the way that I like things to be. I know that I don't usually go out of my comfort zone much at all anymore. And I'm *definitely* not going to do a minute's worth of yoga while I'm there, but...if I'm being honest, I'm pretty curious about the place, actually.

I lean back in my seat, and I fall asleep again, because—hey—I'm on vacation.

I wake up with a start as we touch down in Denver, Colorado. I can't believe that I actually slept through the entire plane ride and descent, but I must have been pretty tired. The plane taxis and docks successfully, and when the "fasten seat belts" sign goes off, I stand, stretching overhead, working at the knots in my shoulders with my fingers. I take down my carry-on from the overhead bin, realizing as I do so that I'll have to take a cab all the way to Boulder from Denver. My mind's starting to go a million miles a minute as I consider my options.

I head out of the secure area of the airport into the regular section, and as I do, I'm struck by the fact that I haven't been to Denver in a very long time. I used to like coming to Colorado for the hiking—I loved the mountains here—and I came about twice a year just for the experience, staying at little hotels that were total holes in the wall, but that were close to some of the best hiking trails.

I realize, a little uncomfortably, that I haven't done that in years. That, honestly, I haven't let myself take time just for *me* in years. It's all work, all the time, in my life and that's great—it pays the bills.

But sometimes, in the back of my head, I realize that years and years of my life are passing by without any real enjoyment anymore. I'm stuck in my ways, I know, but if I was being *really* honest with myself...I'm afraid of trying new things. I'm not as tenacious or resilient as I was when I was teenager or even in my early twenties. I was so outgoing and excited about everything and had this real zest for life...

But then a lot of things happened to me in my twenties. I lost my father. I broke up with the girl I thought I'd love forever. I went to school to become a vet. Hard things, all of them, that forced me to realize that life wasn't all journeys and adventures, like I'd previously imagined.

But I know I've gone to pretty much the other extreme. My life used to be all fun, and now?

Now it's all work.

I've never been particularly good at "balance."

As I walk down the big, bright hallway of the airport, pulling my silent suitcase behind me, I know without a doubt that my sister was right. I really do need this weekend. I might just spend the whole time eating and watching shows on cable...but even if that's all I do, it'll be the most I've let myself relax in a very long time.

And that alone will be worth it.

As I'm walking toward the far entrance to the airport, I'm heading toward the wall of drivers holding signs with scribbled names and people waiting for their loved ones to arrive. What surprises me is that, in that whole muddle of people and signs...I spot my name.

I stop in front of the tall woman with long, red hair holding the sign with my name on it, a clearly lettered "Trisha Dalton." She's dressed in a traditional chauffeur's uniform, and is wearing shades (inside the building) beneath her smart, black cap.

"Trisha Dalton?" the woman asks me, tilting

her head to the side as she pushes her glasses down to the edge of her nose with a warm smile.

I glance up at the woman in surprise. "Yes?" I tell her, suddenly sure she's looking for another Trisha Dalton.

"Wonderful! I'm Reese Edwards—I'm from the Rainbow Yoga Retreat Center, here to pick you up?"

I stare at the woman, blinking. "Wow...sorry..." I tell her, scrambling. "I...uh, I didn't know there'd be anyone here for me," I tell her while Reese bends forward, picking up my suitcase easily.

"That's an oversight on our part," she tells me warmly. "Your secretary was in conversation with us, but we've never spoken with you ourselves, it seems. Your sister, Jacqueline Dalton, purchased the exclusive elite package for this weekend for you, so it comes with a lot of...perks," she tells me, her smile warming even more as she tilts her head to the side and angles it toward the door. "Shall we? Do you have any baggage to pick up?"

"No, I just brought this one suitcase with me," I tell her with a small shrug, my mind reeling.

Elite package? *Perks?*

"Oh, fine! Well, let's get started—it's about an hour and forty to the retreat center, and I want to get you there before sundown!" She turns smartly on her heel and begins to move smoothly out of the airport like the building's about to catch fire.

Okay, so I think I should send my sister more than just a thank you card as I race after the tall chauffeur. Seriously—what kind of yoga retreat sends a *chauffeur?*

Outside on the curb waiting for us is a big,

black town car. Reese sets my suitcase in the trunk, and then holds the back door of the car open for me.

I slide inside, and she shuts it behind me.

The car's nice—a really plush interior with soft, smooth jazz playing on the speakers overhead—but I've got a lot of questions.

"So, what's this place like?" I ask Reese when she gets into the driver's seat, shutting the door and buckling her seat belt.

"Rainbow Yoga?" she asks me, glancing mischievously into the rear view mirror and smiling back at me. "Oh, Rainbow Yoga is a *very* special place."

And that's pretty much all I'm able to get out of her for the rest of the ride. She keeps evading all of my questions with polite deference and maddening nonchalance. I know I've probably misjudged this place, but seriously! I've never heard of a retreat center that would send a town car an hour and forty minutes to pick up a single participant. That's just crazy, no matter what kind of exclusive package my sister got me.

It's afternoon in Denver, and the sun slicing through the clouds and back lighting the mountains is sublime. It's been such a long time since I saw those beautiful Rockies, and they still take my breath away, even after all these years.

I remember when I was a teenager. I was so sick of how flat Florida is, was so sick of its torturous heat in the summer, how everything was old with peeling paint and kitschy in an often sad way. I wanted to leave Florida as soon as I could. I had what my mother called an "itchy foot." I wanted to travel the world, see everything that could be seen...and, after all that, I actually wanted to end up living in Colorado.

I never really told many people of my plan, but

it was firmly planted in my head. Only Jackie knew about it, my sister keeping it a secret because she knew how precious it was to me, this eventuality. This dream.

And then I got together with Clare.

Clare wanted to move out to Colorado, too, which is what we first started talking about when we met: our mutual love for the mountains. Clare was just as passionate about animals as I was, I learned, and she wanted to start a farm, raise sheep in Colorado, maybe eventually get some horses. As the days passed, as I fell more and more in love with Clare, I realized that I wanted to do all of that with her, beside her. Together.

I blink, taking a deep breath. As we drive towards the mountains, I watch the peaks loom closer and closer, leaving the bright lights and tall buildings of Denver behind us. I really didn't think that this trip would make me so nostalgic. I thought, after all, that this would just be a vacation. But it's dredging up all these old thoughts and feelings...all these old dreams that I stifled, over time, purposefully forgetting them.

Don't get me wrong—I love my job. I *love* being a vet, and I love my clients. I have my favorite animals and people who come in to the office and examining rooms every single day and make that day brighter. I love taking care of animals, love helping them, love easing pain, and love helping their people. Even on the hardest days where I have to assist someone to make the difficult decision to let a loved, furred friend move on in peace, I cherish the knowledge I have, my practice and what I'm capable of.

But staying in Florida was never something I thought I'd do. I came back to my hometown of West Palm Beach after college, and I thought I'd move elsewhere, set up my practice in a different city, a different state. But when I came back home...that was that. It was like my whole life suddenly had a nice, easy road map attached to it, a set path that I'd follow until the day I die.

And I was totally okay with that. I mean, I *am* okay with that. Usually.

I'm just tired. I know that. I'm overworked and I don't get out and do anything fun. When I get back home, I'll make that change. I'll start to run again. Heck, maybe I'll even get back out on the dating scene. Maybe that'd be...nice.

As I watch the mountains come closer, I feel myself relax back into the plush seats of the car. It's pretty excessive and ridiculously luxurious, to be in the back seat of a chauffeured car, but I'd be lying if I said I wasn't enjoying it.

When was the last time I let someone else take the wheel?

The skies darken as we begin the drive up the closest mountain. The hair pin turns on the road are executed professionally, and I don't feel jostled around in the back of the car at all. The high cliffs surrounding us and the steep drop offs are enough to turn anyone's stomach, but it's getting dark, so I don't need to look too closely at any of them, instead staring out of the windshield at the pavement illuminated by the headlights.

When we turn off the main road (if that collection of severe curves could have even been *considered* a main road), and onto a gravel drive, I sit up straight in the back seat. I can't wait to catch that first glimpse of Rainbow Yoga, because now? Now I realize that I really don't have any idea what to expect.

Between the tall firs, I begin to see bits of light ahead. It's hard to make out exactly what I'm seeing in the twilight on the mountains, so I sit back in my seat and do my best to drum up a little more patience.

And then, finally, Reese pulls up in front of Rainbow Yoga.

"Welcome!" she tells me brightly over her shoulder. She gets out of her seat, shutting the driver's side door firmly behind her.

I stare up at the place.

Wow. Very, *very* nice.

The gorgeous, sprawling house is essentially one enormous log cabin, the walls made of beautiful logs that, to my limited knowledge, look hand-hewn. The retreat center has huge, floor-to-ceiling length windows that take in the purple light of dusk on the mountain. I can see a fire burning in an enormous stone fireplace inside, and the wooden chandeliers overhead—everything's very rustic—are turned low. The lighting inside the building, from what I can see, is all turned low, actually, sort of setting the mood. Probably setting it for romance (it *is* a singles retreat), which makes me have a little trepidation, butterflies fluttering in my stomach, but then I remind myself again: I'm probably staying in my room relaxing all weekend.

And, even if I wasn't, the likelihood of a single lesbian showing up to this thing—besides me—is really improbable. In the "totally not going to happen" category, actually.

Reese opens the door for me, and I step out of the car, wincing as I stand upright—my back's been bothering me for weeks now. She takes the suitcase out of the trunk, and then turns to smile at me. "Shall we?" she asks, and we both start up the wide, wooden steps toward the big glass front doors.

Even with all of the enormous windows and the wide open views of the mountains, the place actually looks cozy. Maybe it's the roaring fire in the reception area, or the warm, plush couches that look so soft I want to sink down into them. The warmth, coupled with the splendor of the outdoors, is so gratifying and soul-satisfying that I can feel any remaining tension I had in me about the weekend begin to dissipate.

Reese sets my bag down beside me, reaches forward and taps the bell on the oak counter. She tips her hat to me with her wide smile, and turns on her heel, heading back outside and to the car.

I shiver a little, drawing my coat closer about me. It was miserably cold outside, but the snow...the snow is *beautiful*...

"Hello...you must be Trisha Dalton."

I turn at that warm, low voice, and I take a deep breath.

A woman is striding down the corridor toward me, her full lips pulled up into a dazzling smile. She's about as tall as I am, but that's about where our similarities end. She's muscular and lithe, and both of these facts are made more than obvious by the fact that she's only wearing a deep blue sports bra and very clingy workout pants. Her thick, red mane of hair is swept up in a messy ponytail, and her bright green eyes flecked with amber glitter as she smiles warmly at me.

God...she's so my type. She's actually the type that my knees go completely weak for. She has a sexy, upturned nose; a million freckles dotting her face; long lashes framing those brown-green eyes (with not a scrap of makeup anywhere to be seen) and she has such a perfectly kissable mouth. Her lips, in fact, form the most sublime, sumptuous Cupid's bow I've ever seen. But it's not just that. She has this raw grace about her, this predatory ease in movement.

When she steps out from around the corner, moving toward me, it's like I'm looking at a wolf, prowling down the corridor to meet me.

That's a weird metaphor, but it's the best I've got: she reminds me of a wolf.

"Yes," I tell her then, licking my dry lips because I realize she said "hello" about an entire minute ago, and I've been staring at her like I was born yesterday. Which, I promise you, I wasn't. "I'm Trisha Dalton, but everyone calls me Trish," I tell her, sticking my hand out to her while I smile.

"I'm Kennedy Butler," she tells me, voice low enough that I feel the purr of her words drift over my skin, making me shiver. She smiles, tipping her head to the side, spreading her arms wide as she rocks back on her heels. "It's my pleasure to welcome you, Trish, to my retreat center! We're completely thrilled you could join us for this weekend."

"Wow...you own Rainbow Yoga?" I ask her, and her smile deepens coyly as she tilts her head back, her waterfall of red curls brushing back over her shoulder as she nods.

"It's my pride and joy," she tells me fiercely, and I can see that as her eyes move from me to drift over the reception area and the warm, inviting common room. Her face shines as she takes in what I was just pretty impressed by. Kennedy turns back to me, then, placing her hands on her curvy hips as her eyes now *very* deliberately travel up and down my body.

I feel a *zing* of energy and attraction move through me at the speed of light.

For a long moment, I just stand there blinking, but then speech and thought take over the primal physicality of my body that I've been reduced to.

This Kennedy Butler...I mean, wow. She has so much authority and power radiating off of her, she's practically magnetic. I can feel my body leaning toward her, actually, so I'm probably not that far off.

I nervously shove my hand through my hair, making it probably stick up in a million different directions, like I just got shocked by static.

"So, what brings you to our retreat weekend?" Kennedy asks me warmly then, after she's stopped looking me up and down. She leans backward on the front desk with her elbows so that her chest curves out toward me even more than it was already doing.

Do not stare at her, Trish. *Do not stare.*

Technically, right this moment, I should be utterly honest with Kennedy. I should tell her that my sister bought me this awesome weekend retreat package as a Christmas present. I should tell her that I've never done yoga before, that it's my sister who's into yoga—not me. Maybe I should even be so honest as to tell her that I didn't really want to come on this trip in the first place, that people had to talk me into it because I'm a workaholic. *And I don't know the first thing about yoga.*

"I...I just..." I take a deep breath, hold tightly to my purse strap. "I just needed a vacation," I tell her, letting out a little sigh.

Why didn't I tell her the truth?

"Well, we're really glad you're here," says Kennedy, her head to the side again as she smiles at me, the warmth radiating off of her into me, making my shoulders lower a little, tension easing out of me by degrees.

So, I'm not *exactly* lying to Kennedy. I really did need a vacation. I'm just...not sharing the information that I've never done yoga before in my life.

Because it doesn't matter. After all, I'm not going to be doing a second of yoga while I'm here...

"So, you've come in early," she tells me, reaching behind the front desk and procuring an electronic tablet. She wakes the thing up and scrolls through a document. "Most of your fellow retreat attendees aren't arriving until tomorrow...so you practically have the place to yourself to relax, get settled in." Again she pins me with that bright, emerald gaze, making me go all weak in the knees as she gives me a super soft, indulgent smile.

I've got to remember—my sister bought me the super exclusive package. Kennedy's probably just trying to make me feel at home. She's probably, if I'm being honest, this nice to all of the retreat participants. Why wouldn't she be?

But I can't help my attraction and everything that my body is feeling for Kennedy.

My sister—pretty bluntly—calls it "Need-to-get-laid-itis," and I'm pretty familiar with the condition: strong attraction to an obviously confidant, sexy-as-hell lady. I get "Need-to-get-laid-itis" pretty infrequently, but when it comes on, it's strong and insistent. But this is kind of different. I'm very familiar with the fact that I get attracted to ladies pretty frequently. I'm also highly aware of the fact that I don't have time for anything more than the most casual dating and hook-ups right now with how demanding my job has become.

But, again...what I'm feeling towards Kennedy is

kind of different. Kennedy has a sort of animal magnetism to her movements and expressions and gorgeous body...it's true.

But what's also true is the fact that I'm drawn to her in the kind of way that I'm not usually drawn to anyone.

Physical attraction is one thing. Most people have physical attraction for specific attributes, and I know my type of lady through and through, the kind of woman who will make me weak in the knees, who makes my heart flutter. But when I look at Kennedy, there's something so open and kind about her. I've only been around her for a handful of moments, but she strikes me as someone who is big-hearted, fierce and courageous.

My heart that hasn't really cared about much these past few years, the heart that I very, very carefully concealed and hid away so that all of the pain of my past would feel less painful...begins to stir.

It's really disconcerting, that feeling. I don't honestly know if I like it.

But it's happening, all the same.

"Uh..." I cough a little, feeling the floor begin to reel beneath me. All I've been doing all day is sleeping, but I suddenly feel tremendously tired again. Like everything is too much, the inside of the retreat center too warm, the lights overhead—even though they're dimmed—feel too bright on my eyes.

And Kennedy is a little too much, standing right there in front of me, radiating that animal magnetism like sunshine.

"Um...my room?" I ask her, pushing my shoulders back a little, and standing straighter. I want to sit down on something nice and soft and think about what's just happened to me. "I'd love to see my room," I tell her.

But that's apparently not in the cards.

"Let me check the list and see who you're rooming with," Kennedy tells me, fixing me with that dazzling smile again as she pages to another document on her tablet, turning a little away from me.

I blink.

"Rooming?" I ask her, my heart rate increasing.

"Yes—since this is such an intimate singles retreat this weekend, we've really gone all out. All of our instructors will be paired with each retreat participant, so that yoga can be done upon first waking, and when you get ready for bed," she tells me, her head to the side. Little wrinkles appear on her forehead as she frowns softly. "Did you get a chance to read the web site information? It explained all of this—the info was on the site when you registered—"

"No, no...I didn't read the web site information," I tell her, feeling suddenly very, *very* in over my head.

I have the realization at the exact moment she looks up at me from the tablet with a wide smile.

Oh, shit, I think, swallowing. *I'm going to* have *to do yoga.*

"You're going to be rooming with me!" she tells me triumphantly.

I could never have expected this.

Oh, shit, I think, paling. *Oh, shit. Oh,* shit.

"How much yoga experience do you have, Trish?" she asks me, setting the tablet back under the front desk and taking me in once more, her eyes roaming over my body unabashedly.

None. Absolutely none, I think, panic beginning to

set in.

"Oh, you know..." I tell her, turning my hand around and around as I try to figure out where the hell I'm going with this. *Tell her the truth, you idiot!* I think.

The phone behind the desk rings, and Kennedy holds up her finger with a bright smile. "Five seconds—just let me get this. The instructors are up at the summit of the mountain, preparing for this weekend, and I'm expecting a call from one of them," she says, turning away from me. She picks up the phone. "Rainbow Yoga!" she purrs into the receiver.

I back away from her, sitting down on the edge of one of the couches that I thought looked so comfortable a moment ago. I was right—the big, red couch *is* very comfortable, practically sucking me down into it so that my body is completely held by a soft, warm cushion. But it doesn't give me any comfort right now as I consider how, in a few short moments, I've gotten in completely over my head.

Okay—what the hell was that? Did I really not tell her the truth that I don't know the first *thing* about yoga?

So, I'm completely ashamed to admit it, but here it is: I don't *want* to tell her that I'm painfully clueless. It's absolutely stupid, I'll be the first person to say so, but I don't want to tell her that I'm a complete beginner and have no idea what I'm doing...I don't honestly want to be that vulnerable.

I know Kennedy's going to be *rooming* with me, for heaven's sake. She's going to be my personal instructor. *Surely* she'll realize immediately that I don't know the first thing about any of this, that I've never done a minute of yoga in my damn life...

But, maybe...possibly...I take a deep breath and

gulp.

Maybe I can fake it?

Great, Trish—that's your plan? I give a long sigh as I look out the windows at the big, dark storm clouds, rolling in over the mountains. A couple of heavy, thick flakes drift past the window, and in a few moments, it's hard to see the big, tall spruce tree located a few feet away from the back sliding glass door of the retreat center because of the flurry of snow descending from the sky.

Okay. So, yoga, I think to myself furiously. *How hard can it possibly be?*

I have absolutely no experience with yoga other than seeing some sitcom characters do it, the visuals of people doing yoga in commercials and passing a yoga studio on my way to work every day, women coming out of the studios with their hair up in ponytails, holding on to their yoga bags and to-go coffee cups and chatting together.

I used to run a few years ago, and running is pretty hardcore. In comparison of running, how hardcore can yoga possibly be?

Kennedy gets off the phone, comes out from behind the front desk and crosses the space between us, moving her lithe limbs like she's stalking me, a gorgeous, lethal predator with prey in its sights. I don't know why Kennedy gives me that impression, but her movements are so animalistic, so free and fierce.

I swallow, gulping as she strides toward me, as time seems to slow, her cascade of red curls sliding over her bare shoulder and down the soft, pale skin of her arm...

Keep it together, Trish.

"I apologize for the interruption—that was my

head instructor on the phone. They're communing with the nature on top of the mountain, getting back to their...embracing their animal...um, *guides*, for the weekend..." Kennedy tells me, sinking gracefully down on the cushion beside me. She doesn't skip a beat as I wonder what "animal guides" could possibly mean. Kennedy turns a bright, dazzling smile on me, her head to the side. "Did you say that you wanted to see your room?"

"Yes," I tell her resolutely, standing fast. "I'd love to."

"Well, while I'm at it, I'll give you the grand tour of the retreat center," Kennedy tells me, her mouth curling up at the corners like she's about to share a very important secret with me. "If you'd like?" she asks me, rising and standing next to me, close to me, her hip curling out toward me invitingly.

Does she *realize* how much animal magnetism she has? Good God. I swallow again, nodding politely. "Yes, I'd love a tour," I tell her, my mouth as dry as a desert. I dig around in my purse for the bottle of water I bought at the airport.

"I founded Rainbow Yoga about ten years ago," Kennedy tells me then, gesturing to the front desk, the big windows, the warm, inviting space that we both see spreading out in front of us. Her hands are big and broad, and she has long, tapered fingers ending in very short nails, like she bites them, I realize, feeling my cheeks warm as I try to stop watching her every moment, try to take in the retreat center instead.

Kennedy takes a few steps forward, glancing back at me. "I wanted to create a place in the mountains that would be a sanctuary," she says, lifting one brow. "The outside world can be very hectic. It can be judgmental and harsh. I wanted a place where everyone would be welcome, where everyone would feel safe. So Rainbow Yoga was born."

She strides easily out of the main entrance into a wide side hallway lined with watercolor paintings of the mountains surrounding us. I take my suitcase by the handle and follow along behind her.

And try *very* hard not to stare at her butt.

I feel like I'm seventeen years old again, hormones and desire pouring through me. This isn't really like me. I clear my throat again, try to concentrate on what she's saying as I lift my gaze...

And realize that she'd paused in the hallway, turning back to look at me.

And *totally* caught me staring at her rear.

I feel my cheeks color as red as a stop light as I stop on a dime and bite my lip, watching her expression change.

She was in the middle of saying something about the eco-conscious construction of the building, but she stops cold. And then, Kennedy shakes her head a little. And she actually chuckles, the soft laughter low and velvety.

"Anyway," she tells me, raising a single brow and turning back to continue walking down the corridor. Her lips curve into a very sexy smile. "The practice rooms are just here." She inclines her head toward a divide in the hallway and takes the left branch of the corridor.

Kennedy didn't even really skip a beat. And she didn't comment on the fact that I was staring, either. She seemed, if anything, amused by that fact.

Well, now I just feel stupid. She probably gets stared at all the time, by everyone who comes to the retreat center. Kennedy isn't "beautiful" by magazine standards of beauty...but she doesn't have to be. Kennedy has this raw vitality to her, an animal magnetism, she holds your gaze...of course she gets stared at. And here I am, doing what everyone else does. I sigh deeply, tugging my suitcase behind me in dejection. I've really got to get it together.

I realize that if I can't have time in my room alone, then I definitely need a visit to the bathroom just to regroup. I need to splash some cold water on my face, take a couple of deep breaths and try to calm down all of those aforementioned raging hormones.

Just because I'm on vacation doesn't mean I have license to stare at the hot yoga instructor, I remind myself in a huff. *Really, Trish, who does that?*

"Here's the main practice room—it's the one we'll be using during the duration of the weekend, because it's so intimate." Kennedy says in her low, velvet voice as she pushes the wooden door open and strides inside the echoing space beyond. I leave my suitcase in the hallway and follow her in.

The room has immensely tall ceilings that curl inward at the very peak—it takes me a full minute to realize that the ceiling reminds me entirely of a church's.

There are tall windows every few feet set into the wall, and the floor is oak. There is nothing else in the room besides the colorful light fixtures overhead, spilling warm light into the room.

"It's nice," I tell her, biting at my lip as we turn to exit the room, and I see a stack of yoga mats in the corner. I finger the edge of my collar and tug at it, flashing her a worried smile as we step back into the corridor.

"There's a mess hall just down this way," Kennedy tells me, gesturing to our left. "And then your room is the big suite of the place because of your exclusive package. It's the Rainbow Room. It's right this way."

I follow Kennedy down the long hallway to an l-shaped fork in the corridor. We turn down it, and on the right is a modern-looking oaken door with a silver knob.

"Here's the Rainbow Room," Kennedy tells me warmly, opening the door and stepping back so I can take in the room. I have to brush past her to get into the room itself, something I'm sure she didn't realize I'd have to do, but my upper arm is glancing softly against her breasts for half a second before I can step into the room.

Again, a *zing* of electricity moves through me. I take a deep breath, try to calm the thudding of my heartbeat, and I look up at my surroundings.

Whereas the entrance, common rooms and practice rooms of Rainbow Yoga certainly had a lot of windows...this entire room seems to have walls built entirely out of glass. I stop in the middle of the room, my breath catching in my throat...because the room itself looks out on the grandeur of the mountains ascending around us, the snow falling now at a pretty good clip, but I can still see the view. The room has two low beds built in a very modern style in the middle of the floor, and there's a small, modern-looking oak dresser in the corner. The soft mood lighting is continued here, glowing from overhead in blown-glass fixtures.

Mostly, you just pay attention to the fact that only thin glass separates you from the jaw-dropping beauty of nature all around you.

God...it's beautiful. The beauty of the mountains is so put on display here, boldly, fantastically. It actually makes my heart skip a beat.

"Wow," I whisper, stepping through the room and finally letting go of my suitcase handle. I cross the room to stand in front of the farthest glass wall, the wall that looks out on a copse of fir trees that tower over us, cradling the enormous, gray storm clouds overhead. For a moment, the snow lightens up, and I'm able to get a good look at the angry clouds. It looks like a bad storm is rolling in...

"Do you like the room?" Kennedy asks quietly, her voice soft with pleasure as she takes in my reaction. She's leaning on the door frame now with her left hip, her arms folded loosely in front of her, but she hasn't entered the room with me. Not yet.

She's watching me, I realize. Just like I was watching her.

But...that can't be possible. I'm attractive, in my own way, if I'm your type. I have a few extra pounds, but I think it sits well on me, giving my hips a little extra curve. My short brown hair is always misbehaving, but I think it gives me a sort of devil-may-care look on the good days (on the bad days is another story entirely!). I've got a sharp face with high cheekbones, and friends of mine in high school always told me I looked intense. People now just think I'm constantly worrying about something. Which, I suppose, I am.

But as Kennedy takes me in, her eyes roving over my body again, I realize that—this time—she's not assessing my physical condition or how much yoga I've (not) been doing lately.

125

I'm fairly certain she's looking me up and down because she's appreciating the view.

This has happened to me approximately two times in my life (that I've noticed). Once, when I met Clare, and more recently when I met Barbara, my most recent one night stand, courtesy of the Flamingo, the only lesbian bar in West Palm Beach.

I'd like to point out, right now, for the record: *these kinds of things just don't happen to me.* That sounds a little pessimistic, but I'm being serious. I mean, I guess they used to, once...

I take a deep breath as the realization hits me squarely in the heart: the problem is that, yes, these sorts of things *used* to happen to me. They used to happen when I took more risks. When I went out of my comfort zone to experience something I never had before.

I'll never forget the first time I came to the Rockies. I was fresh out of high school, had only a couple of bucks in my pocket because I'd spent most of my money on the round-trip plane tickets to get there and back home. When I arrived in Colorado, I ended up staying at a tiny campground on the side of a mountain, and that night, I met a woman and took her back to my tent. Just like that. Just like *magic*. It had been wild, that night, and I look back on it with fond memories as an example of all of the crazy stuff I used to be completely capable of. The only problem is...it's been years since then. So many years. I feel, sometimes, that I'm a completely different person, going from devil-may-care and anything-is-possible to play-it-safe and don't-take-risks.

But here I am now, standing in a low-lit room in front of Kennedy. The woman who oozes surety as she leans against the door frame, her whole body relaxed, her head to the side as her bright eyes rake over me, her jaw clenched a little as her eyes begin to darken. I know what desire looks like in another woman, and it's growing in her now.

That hits me squarely in the heart. And, if I'm being honest, in other various lady places.

Outside, the snow starts to flurry, big fluffy flakes spiraling in the wind as they hit the glass of the room's walls, thudding gently against it like small insects. Inside, it's warm and cozy. Too warm, actually, as I tug at my sweater's neck, trying to make it strangle me a little less. I wet my dry lips, pressing my damp palms to my thighs.

I *really* like that Kennedy is staring at me like that. But it's also desperately unnerving. It's been such a long time, and I didn't come here with that in mind, so I didn't exactly bring my A-game, so to speak.

But to deny that I'm incredibly attracted to her would be a lie.

She said there's going to be no one here tonight. So...it's just her and me and snow falling outside and absolutely no place to be.

Dangerous things happen on nights like this.

Wonderful things.

If I let them happen. If I help them happen.

I take a deep breath, letting the adrenaline of all this possibility soar through me. I'm unnerved and nervous and utterly excited, and something is stirring inside of me. Something is waking up.

So before I can second-guess myself, before I can talk myself out of anything, I lift my head, lifting my chin in the process. I narrow my eyes a little, take another deep breath, feeling the warmth of the room pressing down on me as I wrap all of my courage around my spine, trying to remember how easy this used to be for me. I used to be fearless.

I want to be fearless again. If only for one more night.

"Kennedy," I tell her, tasting the syllables of her name as they roll off my tongue. I shiver a little, stand straighter, bracing myself. "Do you want to go...for a walk?" I ask her then, trying to keep my voice as level and low as possible as I take a wild leap and hope I'm picking up all the right signals.

Kennedy's eyes actually widen at that. I guess it is a surprising question, considering the circumstances. And the storm that's just beginning outside. She looks past me at the billowing, blowing snow, blinking.

"Honestly?" she asks me, her head to the side. "You want to go for a walk in this? In the dark? On the mountain?" Her lips are curling up slowly into a disbelieving smile.

"Yes," I tell her, rolling my shoulders back. "I mean," I backpedal, trying to come up with some good reasons to go, "I used to come to the Rockies a lot when I was younger. For the hiking. I...I really love hiking in the snow." And it's true. I do.

Adrenaline continues to pump through me as Kennedy raises a single brow, and I'm pretty sure she's impressed for half a heartbeat as she rocks back on her heels. "Well," she says, hooking her thumbs in the waistband of her workout pants, revealing a little more of her muscled stomach. My heart skips another beat, and I try not to stare. Kennedy's mouth rounds up into a sultry smirk as she tilts her head to the right. "What kind of winter gear did you bring?" she asks me, glancing at my single suitcase with one brow raised.

"I brought a parka. Snow pants. It's enough to keep me warm for a short hike tonight," I promise her.

"I trust you know how cold it can get out there," she tells me, that one brow rising a little higher, her mouth flattening into a line as she watches me for a long moment. But then she shrugs, pushes off from the door frame. "I'd love to go for a hike...if that's what you really want," she tells me then, her voice low as she glances at me through her long black lashes, causing my heartbeat to increase. "Meet me at the entrance in five minutes, and we'll go on that hike, Trish," she tells me, her full lips curling up at the corners again and her eyes glittering with something I can't quite read. But that I like tremendously.

And, God, I *really* love it when she says my name with that smile, like we're sharing a secret.

"Okay," I tell her breathlessly. She closes the door behind her, and then I'm all alone in this glass room. All alone with my thundering heartbeat and the realization that I just set something into motion. Something that I was crazy to start, but that I did anyway, consequences be damned.

We're going to take a snowy walk through the woods...I mean, that's pretty damn romantic...if I've been reading her signals right. I want this. I want this *very* much. And if she wants this too, then...possibly...it could actually happen.

Oh, my God. *This could actually happen.* Her. Me. Together. Just like the old days. I take a deep breath, pressing my hand to my heart and feeling my heartbeat thrum beneath my fingers. But I can't think about it too much. That's my problem. I think about *everything* too much, and then the actions I make aren't natural. They're calculated. And I never used to calculate anything. I used to just follow my heart, take the leap and plunge and hope like there was no tomorrow.

And it always ended up working out for me. I have to remember that. Every time I took the leap, things worked out. Maybe not exactly as I would have planned them, but what in life does? No matter what, every time I found enough courage to try something extraordinary, something magical would happen.

I have to remember that.

There aren't any curtains in the room, but—thankfully—there's an on suite bathroom that is *not* built entirely of glass. I'm able to close the bathroom door and have complete privacy as I struggle out of my travel clothes and into my long johns, pulling my turtleneck over my head and over the long johns as the heat blasts into the small room. I'm already sweating as I pull on my parka, not zipping it up, pulling on my snow pants as I pant, chugging water from my bottle. I pause in the mirror after tugging my hat down over my ridiculously messy hair. Kitted out like this, I look a little bit like the Stay Puft Marshmallow Man. I tug at the incredibly puffy sleeves of my parka and make a face at myself in the mirror. Actually, I look like I'm about to embark on an arctic expedition, but that's not that far from the truth.

I make my way out of the bedroom, and I actually manage to make my way back to the reception area without taking a wrong turn. I pause a little way down the corridor just before hitting the common area because my palms are sweating inside of my gloves, not *entirely* because I'm overheated indoors under all this gear. My palms get a bit sweatier, because Kennedy's in the reception area, standing in the entryway, waiting for me.

She's braided her hair in two enormous red braids that hang down her back, with a thin, knitted hat over her ears. She's wearing thin winter gear in varying shades of blue and is leaning easily on the front desk with her elbows, her right leg cocked beneath her as she pages through something on the electronic tablet.

I haven't made a sound. I know I haven't. But whether it's from instinct or because she felt me watching her, Kennedy straightens just then and glances down the corridor at me. She smiles when she sees me, her full lips parting to reveal dazzling white teeth. Kennedy stands straight, looping her blue scarf one more time over her shoulders as she inclines her head.

"Hey, you," she tells me, lifting her chin, her eyes sparkling. "Are you ready for an easy walk in our balmy weather?" she asks me, chuckling a little at her joke.

"Yeah," I tell her breathlessly, waddling down the rest of the hallway in my snow pants, suddenly feeling incredibly overdressed. And, God, do I feel unsexy. Cold weather gear has gotten a bit better and markedly less like the Stay Puft Marshmallow Man in recent years, I'm noting, as I gaze at Kennedy's body in the thin material of her jacket and pants.

Huh. The closer I get, the more I realize that what she's wearing isn't exactly a jacket and snow pants.

It's more like a fleece pullover and jeans. The dim light overhead is hard to see by, but it's obvious...she's not dressed for a hike on the mountains in winter.

"Um...are you going to go get dressed?" I ask her, gesturing with my gloved hand at her clothes. "I can wait here, if you like—"

"Oh, no, I'm all set," she tells me, pushing off from the front desk and licking her lips as she narrows her eyes and glances back at me. "Are you all ready? You think you'll be warm enough?"

"Says the woman in the jeans and pullover," I quip back, then realize that I just joked with this woman like I've known her for a lot longer than a handful of moments. But it came naturally, that bit of joking, and I liked it.

It seems that she did, too, because she laughs now, a rich, warm sound that I like very much, feeling the sound of her laughter roll over me and warm me even more. But this warming I like. Kennedy chuckles, throwing her head back, her red braids sliding over her shoulders like her hair is made of satin. I'd like to test that, actually, feel that hair sliding over my own skin...but I try to push that from my mind as Kennedy shakes her head.

"All right, you got me. Fair enough. The cold doesn't bother me," she tells me with an elegant shrug. "But let's get going before the snow starts coming down even thicker, yeah?" she tells me, jerking a thumb toward the front door.

"Okay, but you're *really* just wearing that? All joking aside, you're going to freeze your socks off," I mutter as we make our way toward the front door. Kennedy opens that door, holding it open for me as I pass through the veil of heat into the frigid tundra that is the great outdoors.

"It's actually warm out today. You know. For the time of year that it is," Kennedy tells me with a little wink.

I blink at her, feeling my eyeballs beginning to freeze.

That's...really not true.

As much as I felt overdressed inside, in a matter of *seconds* I feel vastly, *vastly* underdressed to be out here. The wind pierces me through, even pummeling the cold through the thick layers of my parka and underclothes. The wind is violent, driving snow slant-wise into my face and the tiny bit of exposed skin between the cuffs of my gloves and the cuffs of my jacket. I tug my jacket sleeves down a little more and tremble inside of my layers.

Cold used to not bother me at all. But then I didn't leave Florida for a couple of years. And that changes you, constantly going from warm to *really* warm and never having to deal with the cold. Yeah, there were occasional nights where the temperature got down to a "freezing" forty degrees in West Palm Beach, but those were very, *very* rare occurrences (that were then talked about among my clients for months afterward). It just doesn't get that cold in Florida, and I lost whatever made me capable of dealing with very cold temperatures because I never left my state.

I shiver inside of my parka, glancing sidelong at Kennedy, who is standing exactly as she was inside, shoulders back, chin lifted, confidant. She doesn't look like she even feels the cold, which is just crazy. She shoves her hands into her fleece's pockets and shoots me a warm smile, her head to the side a little as she flicks her gaze towards the woods. "So, do you want a short trail or a long trail?" she asks me, not even raising her voice over the whistling winds that begin to pummel us. "Did you have dinner before you made it up the mountain?" she asks.

"The short trail sounds nice," I tell her, my chattering teeth making the words sound a little

133

staccato. "And no, I didn't have dinner."

Kennedy nods. "One of our instructors is our cook. She's very top notch—you'll love her food—but, unfortunately, she's also up the mountain with the other instructors preparing for the retreat tomorrow. So it's just my cooking you'll have to contend with for tonight, I'm afraid. I'm not very good, but I can microwave a mean dinner," she tells me. And then she winks with a little chuckle, turning as she sets off down what I assume to be a trail. But it's only an arbitrary path in the thick snow that she's making, her long legs making her stride easily through the snow like it's not even there. I have no choice but to follow her.

As we walk toward the trees, we're eventually swallowed up by their tall bulk and immense shadows, stepping from the clearing around the retreat center into the woods. The minute we're beneath the trees, the snow and wind becomes a little lessened, and I can actually see in front of me again without narrowing my eyes against the relentless, driven snow. I relax a little, now that the cold is gentled a bit, and I watch Kennedy striding ahead of me.

She moves with such surety and grace. I've walked in knee-high snow before. I know it's tough slogging out ahead of me, but she's plowing through it like it's nothing to her. She's still just in her fleece and jeans, by the way, one light hat on her head, her long, red braids hanging down behind her. The snow on the ground makes everything pretty light out, and I can see easily on this night walk. I watch her legs as she plows through the snow, the muscles in her thighs flexing easily. I watch her shoulders that she curves forward, focused wholly on her task, her head bent, her face in profile as we round a bend in the trail.

My heart skips a beat again, and I take a deep, cold breath.

Kennedy looks so natural out here, I realize. Like she's part of the woods herself. I'm a little surprised by that thought, but watching her move gracefully between the trees, moving through the snow like she's striding on a sidewalk downtown, I'm struck by how true it is. She completely looks like she belongs out here. Weird.

"How long have you lived in Colorado?" I find myself asking her. Once the words come out of my mouth, I'm mentally kicking myself. Smooth, Trish. Real smooth. I could have started with "do you come here often," and it'd be less obvious.

Kennedy glances back at me over her shoulder and pauses in her wading through the snow. "I've lived here my whole life," she tells me with a graceful shrug. "These mountains are in my blood," she tells me, casting back a gentle smile. "What about you? Where do you live?"

"Florida," I tell her with a little chuckle.

She frowns a little, shaking her head. "Oh, good God, you must be so cold...are you all right out here?"

"No, no, I'm fine," I totally lie. "I mean, I used to come to the Rockies all the time when I was younger," I say, shrugging. "You know," I tell her, gulping down the freezing air. I glance up at the trees, at the lightly falling snow. "I actually thought I was going to live here once," I find myself telling her.

"Wow, really?" she asks me. She takes her hands out of her pockets and tucks a stray curl of red behind her ear before she continues deeper into the woods. "So what happened?" She glances back at me over her shoulder with a small grimace. "What made you change your mind?"

My walking slows for a moment. "Well," I say, breathing out into the cold. My breath fogs in front of me like smoke. "I mean, a lot of things happened all at once, but the two most important really did me in..." I take another deep breath, feeling my pulse begin to pound a little faster. "See," I mutter, the words coming out faster now, "I broke up with the woman I thought I'd spend the rest of my life with. And then my father passed away right after that." God, it's still hard to say that. It's still so damn hard. I close my eyes for a moment, curl my hands into my fists. When I open my eyes, I'm a little calmer, a little more subdued. "It was just a brutal time for me," I tell her quietly. "So I stopped wanting it. I started focusing on my studies instead."

After a long moment of silence in which Kennedy doesn't give any sort of reply, we continue to slog through the snow. I clear my throat then, feeling my cheeks flush. "Sorry," I say with a little cough, embarrassment rolling over me in waves. "I'm sorry, that was kind of heavy, and—"

"No," Kennedy tells me, glancing over her shoulder at me and shaking her head. She pushes her hands deeper into her pockets, bending her head toward the ground, her breath curling out into the air around her face. "No, *I'm* sorry. I was just thinking about my parents. I lost them both together, so I completely understand." Her words are soft and heavy, like the big flakes of snow that settle gently to the ground. "I was trying to think of something comforting to say," she tells me, her voice going deeper. Quieter. She breathes out, turns toward me, her eyes dark. "But there's never really anything *comforting* you can say to that. Not truly. But I am very sorry, Trish."

"Wow. Both of your parents...God, I'm so sorry." I shake my head, wrapping my arms around me. I'm still for a moment before I say: "I'm...I'm really lucky—and I know I'm lucky—that I still have my mother," I say quietly. "Kennedy, I'm really sorry."

Kennedy takes a deep breath, her eyes lightening as she flicks a gaze to me and then away. "Honestly, yoga is what helped me deal with it," she says then, lifting her chin and glancing up at the trees that tower all around us, at the gently falling snow that spirals down between the trunks, falling between us soundlessly.

I look at her in surprise. "Really?" I ask her, unable to help myself. "I mean, isn't yoga just an exercise?"

Kennedy glances back at me then, her eyes hooded and her face set in a very soft smile. "Yes. Yoga's definitely an exercise, and an awesome one at that. But it's so much more." She shrugs, leaning toward me. We're close enough now that when we both breathe out together, the ghosts of our breath merge in the darkening air. "When you're in the middle of a difficult yoga pose," she tells me, her voice low and warm, her eyes glittering in the dark, "when you're asking your body to stretch and loosen up, when you're in that moment where it's just you and your breath and your body...you're *right here*." She reaches up slowly, her long fingers reaching across the space between us...and she presses her hand against my heart.

Her palm isn't *exactly* against my heart—there's, admittedly, quite a few layers between my skin and hers.

But still—it's such an intimate gesture that it kind of blows me away. Suddenly, just like she said (even though I'm fairly certain I'm not doing a yoga pose at the moment), I'm right here. I'm right here with her. It's just Kennedy and me beneath the trees, in the snow. Kennedy, touching my heart.

My heart that skips a beat, right at that moment.

My blood pounds through me as Kennedy holds my gaze with her intense eyes. For a long moment we say absolutely nothing. But I feel everything. I feel that it's one of the most intense things I've ever done, taking this chance, coming on this vacation, coming on this walk with Kennedy tonight. But I did it. I'm here. I'm experiencing this.

And it's beautiful.

Kennedy takes another deep breath, and she slowly, almost regretfully, drops her hand down to her side. My legs go a little limp when she's no longer touching me, but I stiffen my knees, shove my hands into my coat pockets, take a deep breath and try to stand a little straighter.

"Yoga brings you back into yourself," she tells me quietly then. "It makes you right here, right in this moment. And there's nothing else besides you and your breath and your connection to something you can't exactly see, but you feel with your heart. It's sublime, that feeling." Kennedy watches me for a long moment, her eyes dark and impossible to read. "And it was that feeling that reminded me that my parents are never truly gone. That they're still with me, even though I can't see them or hear them or touch them anymore." She reaches up and places her bare hand over her left breast, her fingers trailing down her fleece jacket for a moment. "They're still here, because they're still in my heart."

Coming from anyone else, I would think that that last statement would almost sound corny or saccharine. But as we pause beneath the falling snow, as we look into one another's eyes, I know that she just said this from the deepest part of her heart. That she means it utterly. And that vulnerability in that moment...it honestly takes my breath away.

An hour ago, we were complete strangers, but here we are, in the dark woods, telling each other hard things, telling each other the hard parts of the stories of our lives. I don't often do this. I'm never this vulnerable, usually, to anyone. Not even my sister, really, the person I'm closest to in this entire world. She knows how much I miss Dad. But I don't think she knows, not really, what his death did to me, how I gave up everything I really loved, after he died. How my life changed.

"Hey," Kennedy tells me, her voice low as she gazes into my eyes, cocking her head gently to the left. "Are you all right?"

I take a deep breath. I close my eyes. I dredge up every bit of courage I have in me. "I'm sorry," I tell her then, letting out my breath in a long sigh. "I have no idea why, but coming on this vacation...it's done something to me. It's made me think of all the ways I've changed, since my father's death." The words come out very small, escaping into the air between us: "I don't really know if I like who I've become," I tell her.

Once the words are out of my mouth, I have immediate regret. I can't believe I just told her that, the person I've found so deeply sexy and amazing. I told her something so vulnerable and painful about myself,

139

and now...now I can't take it back. It's out in the open between us.

Kennedy reaches up slowly, gently, like she's about to touch a wild animal, and any fast movements might startle it. But she's not touching a wild animal. She's reaching up, and then she's pressing her palm against my cheek, cupping my cheek and jaw against her hot skin.

And she is hot, hot like she's burning up, like she's feverish. But it's *so cold* out here. How is that possible?

"You know what I've learned lately?" she tells me then, breathing the words out.

"What?" I ask her, trembling from the cold or her touch...I'm not entirely certain.

Kennedy gazes at me quietly. "At any moment," she tells me, her beautiful lips forming the words as I watch them intently, "we can begin again."

For a long moment, I feel the truth of her words. And, God, I want to believe them. I want to believe them *so badly*. But I can't. I can feel the tears start, but I squelch them, taking a deep breath. And then I take a step back, and the moment is lost, falling away from us like the snow as her hand loses contact with my skin. "I'm sorry," I tell her, wrapping my arms around me again as I shake my head. My words sound hollow. "I'm just not sure if I believe that," I tell her, feeling regret burn through me.

The problem is that I'm filled with *so much regret*. Regret for the fact that I gave up my dreams. Regret that my father's death forced me into a life that he would have never wanted for me. I think he knew that I didn't want to stay in Florida. He supported, so much, my frequent trips to the Rockies, could never get enough of the pictures I took, just to show him how beautiful it was there.

Here.

I think my father secretly wanted to leave Florida, too. He wanted adventures, wanted the thrill of something different. He was waiting for retirement, and then he and Mom were going to buy the RV that they'd been saving for, take off together and see everything they'd planned. They were going to start in Florida, of course, go to all of the kitschy, wonderful tourist stops that are still in operation. And then...the sky was the limit. They were going to see all of America, my father told me proudly.

And then it couldn't happen anymore. He'd never get the chance. Because he was gone.

Kennedy stays silent for a long moment, standing tall and quiet, the snow falling all around us in a hush. She lifts her chin, her hands easily at her sides, her eyes glittering in the dark.

She looks so wolf-like standing there. Not in a scary way, though I'm fully cognizant of the fact that wolves can be pretty frightening. But then, there's really never been an animal I was afraid of. And yes, Kennedy's wolf-like, standing there...but the comparison is one of beauty. She looks, honestly, noble.

My heart's beating hard again, and I'm pretty emotional in this moment. I'm thinking about Dad, about all of the things he wanted to do but never got a chance to. I'm thinking about all of the regrets I've had in my own life, so many, many more than I can possibly count. I'm thinking of all of the times I said "no" when I desperately wanted to say "yes." All those times that I didn't take chances because I wanted to be safe.

But it's not safe, what I'm doing right now, going for a walk in the night on the mountain, the snow falling down around us, the cold so visceral, I feel it in my bones.

I watch Kennedy and Kennedy watches me.

"The thing is," I tell her, fear pouring through me. I push through it anyway. I stand as tall as I can, and though I'm shaking (not from the cold this time, I'm certain of it), I *push through the fear anyway*. And I take a deep breath and tell her: "I want to believe I can start again," I whisper to Kennedy. "But...I don't know how."

Something flickers across Kennedy's face again, and—her eyes dark and hooded—she takes a step toward me. I stand my ground, even though everything in me—all of the "safe" impulses that I've built up over the years that keep me from ever moving outside of my comfort zone and trying anything wonderful—is firing on all cylinders. I stand perfectly still, my knees locked stiff, my skin shivering, and I hold my breath as Kennedy reaches up again, as—again—she cups her hand to my cheek and chin, her hot palm resting against my skin, creating a fire in me that is unquenchable.

"Nobody knows how to start over, Trish," she says softly, gently. "You just *try*. You hope like crazy. But you try. And if it doesn't work," she whispers, her eyes glittering, "you try again."

The surety of that statement hits me square in the heart. I feel how true it is through my whole body, to the deepest part of my bones and back again.

And I know, in that moment, that I believe it. That I believe *her*.

The air is sparking between us, electricity rushing over my skin as want and desire flood through me. Because, in this moment, I've opened the gates...

I've let myself feel the totality of how much I want Kennedy.

And instead of talking myself out of it, instead of telling myself that it's not safe to do this, that I'm setting myself up for heartache to do this, that—for a million reasons—I *shouldn't* do this...

I do it anyway.

I...try.

My heartbeat is thundering through me so loudly that it's all I can hear, my blood rushing like a spring about to be flooded. If I don't do it right this damn minute, I'm going to lose all my nerve. So I just do it. I take the final step that's separating Kennedy and me. I take that step, and then my enormous, puffy parka is pressing against her front, and I'm reaching out and curling my fingers over her hips, hooking my thumbs in her jeans belt loops. There's electricity seemingly crackling between my hands and her as I draw our bodies even closer together, pulling us closer, as close as we can get with my winter gear separating us.

And I tilt my chin up, my nose brushing against hers.

And we stay like that for only half a heartbeat. Because I wanted her to want this to, I wanted to know that I hadn't misread the signals. That I'm still capable of wanting someone who wants me just as much. That I can still recognize how I feel without squashing it down, and that I can still act on it.

I wanted her to want me.

And she does.

Kennedy brings her hands up to my hips, too, drifting her palms up and over my back until her strong arms are wrapped around my shoulders, drawing me even closer to her. We meet at the exact same time, our lips brushing against one another, gentle for just a heartbeat, and then full of intensity and need, soft and hot all at once.

The electricity that has been crackling all over my skin roars through me like a bolt of lightning as we kiss each other now. I shudder against Kennedy as the electric kiss devours the both of us in waves of need. This is not a simple little kiss. This is energy, this is want and desire as our lips merge, as our tongues entwine, hers sneaking into my mouth even as I smile against her, breathing out in a hiss of want.

Kennedy leans away from me, and—for a second—I'm worried that this wasn't what it seemed. I feel cold as she leans away, but then I see her staring down at me, her eyes dark with desire.

"Do you want to cut the walk short?" she asks me, her voice in a low growl as she digs her fingers into my hips.

It takes me only a second to recognize what's implied in that statement.

Do you want to cut the walk short? can be translated to *want to come back to my place?*

"Yeah," I murmur, stepping away from her, the world shaking as I whisper it out between us. *Yes to everything.* I run a hand through my hair, the electricity still crackling between us.

She stares at me for a long moment, flexing her fingers, and then her mouth curls up at the corners as she ducks her head down a little, staring at me through her long black lashes.

"Shall we?" she murmurs, and, elegantly...gracefully...Kennedy turns and bows a little, gesturing back the way we came, gazing up at me with hooded eyes darkened with desire, eyes that shake me to my core.

My heart in my throat, I move past her slowly, feeling time seem to slow down as I pass her, her eyes on me, roving over me. Even though I'm wearing this enormous parka and pair of snow pants...it doesn't seem to matter to her. Everything that I am, physically, is hidden away by enormous snow gear...but there's still lust and want in Kennedy's face as she gazes after me. Like she knows what lies beneath, under the gear.

Like she knows what's inside of me, what makes me....*me*. And she likes it very much.

Electricity continues to crackle over my skin, as together, about a foot from one another, we make the slog back toward the retreat center through the broken snow of the path we already made. My heart is thrumming inside of me, and everything that I am feels electrified, yes. But also confused.

It seems like we're heading back to...I don't know. I think it's pretty obvious that we're going to go back to our room together. Kennedy strides ahead of me now in the night, and it's hard to tell exactly what she's thinking.

Normally, right now, I'd do a million second guesses. I'd talk myself out of what just happened, say that I'd missed the signals, even though I know they were there. Even though I know that what we're heading back to the retreat center for is *not* some yoga. I'd try to tell myself that I shouldn't do this. I'd come up with a million reasons why this wasn't a good idea (even if I believed, utterly, that it *was* a good idea), because this has become so far outside of my comfort zone.

But the truth of the matter is that, many years ago now, I did things like this without thinking about the consequences. I took my risks, and somehow—always—it all turned out okay.

Okay, so yes...this might all turn out horribly. Kennedy is the owner of the retreat center. Anything could happen, and I could get hurt, or I could hurt her. I don't deny that.

But...what if we didn't hurt one another? What if the attraction I've felt for Kennedy is mutual? What if something *wonderful* is about to happen to me?

Normally I wouldn't weigh the positives. I'd never take the risk in the first place.

But for tonight—just for tonight—I'm trying. And I'm going to take that risk, come what may.

I thought we'd walked a lot farther than this, but it's only a handful of moments until we reach the retreat center again. The light is still soft and subdued inside, and when the front door gives beneath Kennedy's hand, I realize my heart is in my throat.

I take a deep breath as Kennedy holds the door open for me.

And then I step inside.

Inside the entrance, it's warm and quiet. I can hear the heat coming on throughout the building as we let in the cold air, but other than that, all is silent. Kennedy closes the door behind me, and I take off my hat, threading my fingers through my hair, probably making it stand up in a million directions. But I don't care.

I turn, my breath coming quickly, as I gaze back at Kennedy.

She's leaning against the door with one shoulder, gazing at me quietly, her eyes dark. The entryway is much dimmer lit than the reception area, but still—I can see the desire in her eyes.

I don't say anything. And neither does she. Instead, I unzip my parka, stepping forward and letting it slide in a puddle of melting snow to the ground. I peel out of my snow pants, letting the straps slide over my shoulders, and then I'm stepping out of those, too.

It's really, really far from a super sexy strip tease, but now I'm in my long johns, and Kennedy is stepping forward, wrapping her hands around my hips again. I tug at the zipper at her throat, pulling it down to open up the fleece pullover. There are so many layers we have to maneuver through, but we're getting there. Kennedy chuckles as I pull the fleece over her arms, and I'm chuckling, too, when she hooks her fingers into the waistband of my long johns.

"Where's the driver—Reese?" I ask her, beginning to pant as Kennedy crouches down in front of me, slowly tugging the waistband of the long johns down, then dragging the fabric over the skin of my thighs and my knees until they're a puddle of fabric on the floor, and I'm just wearing my turtleneck and panties.

"She's probably in the mess hall," she tells me, glancing up with one brow up, her lips turned into a sexy smirk. "But she won't bother us. She won't come here."

"What?" I ask her, my breath coming out even faster as Kennedy hooks her thumbs now into the waistband of my panties, still perfectly balanced in front of me in a crouch, her thigh muscles quite evident through her thin jeans.

"She won't bother us, I promise you," Kennedy says, her voice rich and low and sultry as she begins to slowly, tantalizingly, pull down my panties.

"No," I tell her then, reaching down, holding her hands tightly against my hips. Kennedy glances up instantly, her face darkening with concern.

"Are you all right?" she asks me, licking her lips. "I can stop right now. I'm sorry, I thought—"

"No, no, I want this," I tell her. *God*, I want this. I glance around, shaking my head. "Just...not here. Not where someone could see us."

Kennedy's mouth turns up at the corners again as she rises fluidly, her hands leaving my hips. "If I promised you," she says, leaning over me, bringing her arms around me tightly, "that we wouldn't be interrupted...would you believe me? I promise that Reese has a sort of...animal instinct...about things. She won't bother us—"

"But you can't promise me that," I tell her, shaking my head, my breath coming fast. "She could show up at anytime for any reason. Let's just go to the room, okay?"

Kennedy's lips turn up at the corners so beautifully that, for a heartbeat, she takes my breath away. "As you wish," she murmurs to me, leaning forward and brushing her full, warm lips against my left temple.

I shudder against her, and then I'm grabbing up my wet parka and snow pants and long johns, and I'm following after her down the corridor as she leads the way to the bedroom—the bedroom that, I realize, I would never be able to find the way back to if she wasn't directing me. Her hand is blazingly hot against my palm as she threads her fingers through mine, pulling me gently down the hall after her.

Once we're inside the bedroom, once the door

is closed behind us, I let the parka and pants fall to the floor in a wet heap. I pull my turtle neck up and over my head, and then my long john shirt follows. I'm standing there in my bra and panties now, and Kennedy is lifting her chin, is breathing out and stepping forward.

We meet each other in front of the door, wrapping our arms around each other, drawing the other close, close, closer still, our hips pressing tightly together, our breasts together, our mouths, at last, meeting again in a fevered kiss. She is all warmth and softness and desire as I kiss her deeply, desperately, drinking in the heat of her mouth as she moans against me, a deep, guttural sound that sounded—just for a heartbeat—like a growl. A thrill races through me, a shudder, as I place my palms against the small of her back, under her shirt, tracing my fingers over her skin.

There are no consequences to this right now, I realize. Right in this moment, right in this very moment, there's nothing but Kennedy and I, the quietness of the retreat center, the snow hitting the glass walls all around us, and the pine trees rising just beyond the glass walls, stately and still. There are just our two bodies, our two hearts pressed against one another.

I want this. I want her. And she wants me. And, right now, right at this one, perfect moment...everything is right with the world.

So we come together in this space, the two of us, with the light turned low overhead, with the two modern beds set up in the center of the room. I turn Kennedy, my hands guiding her hips, until her legs press back against the edge of the closest bed. Together we both fall onto the bed, Kennedy on her back, me on top of her, straddling her.

We're both chuckling as we land, bouncing, on top of the mattress. But then I'm kissing her mouth again, capturing it with my own, lingering over her lips, her tongue, as I drink her in. I kiss her jaw now, tracing a pattern of kisses down her neck to her clavicle, trying a taste of her skin now, my tongue drawing a sweet, wet spiral over her right breast. Kennedy shudders beneath me, the laughter no longer coming from her mouth. Instead, she pants against me, arching up beneath me. I undo the button of her jeans, tugging down the zipper and then tugging the pair of pants off of her entirely, sliding the material over her legs, grabbing her socks with it.

Wow. For a long moment I stare down at her, and then tentatively, cautiously, I begin to trace the muscles of her legs with the tips of my fingers. She watches me carefully from beneath hooded eyes, her elbows digging into the bed beneath her as she stares up at me, her breath coming out in long, sharp exhales.

"God, you're...you're *amazing*," I whisper to her, bending over her, bending my head down and capturing her mouth again. My hands trace her muscles, learning the sculpture of them as she smiles against my mouth, wrapping her arms around my neck and bringing me down until I'm lying fully on top of her, embracing her with my entire body as she wraps her legs around my hips, as her center presses against me.

"So are you," she whispers to me, then, her lips against my neck as I crouch above her, as I stare down at her, into her, gazing into her eyes as my fingers learn every inch of her.

I want to watch her as I touch her, want to watch her reactions as my fingers connect with the very center of her. So I do. I trace my fingertips down the front of her belly, over her hips and between her thighs, underneath the fabric of her panties, smoothing my fingers against her center. She closes her eyes, gasping out, arching beneath me as I stroke slowly, gently, tantalizingly, her wetness.

Out of her mouth, again, comes a low, deep growl. It's so animalistic in its intensity that, for a heartbeat, I almost falter in my touch. But I don't. The depth of the growl makes my skin shiver with excitement, makes me press down harder against her center as I rise above her, kissing her again, my lips finding new paths to trace now, as I kiss a patterned spiral down the front of her body, teasing her right breast now, as I kiss around the nipple. I lick it gently—it's so firm in my mouth, against my tongue, as she growls beneath me, her hands in my hair now, pressing down insistently, encouraging me to kiss her harder. And I do. I kiss her nipple, teasing it between my teeth gently now, and then I bite down, not too hard, but hard enough, as her hips buck up to meet my hand, my hips. I grind down against her with my hips, my hips at her center, and she wraps her legs around me, pressing herself against me.

We move together, finding the rhythm that we both need, that we're both desperate for, in these moments.

"I need you," she whispers to me, her eyes glittering in the dim light. She wraps her fingers around my wrist, pressing my hand down harder against her. Desire roars through me as I curl my fingers, bringing them into her as she shudders against me, as she arches her back, her mouth open in a perfect expression of need. I love that I'm making her feel like that, and as I press against her, into her, I learn what makes her moan, what makes her growl, what makes her move against me in perfect rhythm.

When she shudders beneath me, a sort of primal satisfaction uncurls in my belly. As I listen to her sweet, deep groan of completion, as I feel her shiver in my arms, I feel a type of peace descend over me that I haven't felt in...well.

A very long time.

"God," she whispers after a long moment, as I press a soft kiss to her mouth, to her temple, to her jaw. "God," she whispers again, curling her fingers over my shoulders, drawing me up to kiss her again, meeting her mouth in all its delicious heat and need.

"That felt so good," she whispers to me, catching my eyes, then, her lips glistening, her cheeks flushed. "That felt *so good*," she repeats, her mouth turning up at the corners as she runs a hand through her hair, sitting up on one elbow. She doesn't say anything else, only expertly rises, pushing my hips down against the bed, moving against me until I'm beneath her, she's on top, and her wicked smile is making a shudder of delight race through me.

We don't sleep tonight. At least, not for hours yet. There is a rhythm to be learned, from both of us. There are curves to memorize with fingertips, with kisses. There is love to be made, and—for the space of hours—not a single thought to be had.

I feel everything, in this space. I think of nothing.

And it's wonderful.

As we move together, I'd almost say it's perfect.

When I wake up, I shiver, pulling the blankets up to my shoulders as I sit up, the bed creaking gently beneath me as I sit back on one hand, blinking the sleep from my eyes. Outside, the dark storm clouds have cleared, and the moon overhead is making the snow glitter like a landscape sprinkled with diamonds. The pine trees ascend toward the sky like thin sentinels, the mounds of snow glittering at their feet. And it's so beautiful, out of doors, that—for a brief moment—it takes my breath away.

I shiver again as a soft, cold breeze brushes over the bare skin of my shoulders. For a moment, I'm confused where the chill could be coming from, but then I get my bearings and take in the corner of the room. All of the walls are glass, and—in the corner—there seems to be a doorway of glass to the outside.

That door is open.

I stare at the soft drift of snow that's scuttled into the room, and I realize I must be dreaming. I don't know why—maybe it's the quality of light overhead, the moonlight dazzling on the snow outside. But this feels very dream-like. I pat the bed beside me, and I'm disappointed when my hand touches nothing but cool blanket, sheet and mattress.

Kennedy is gone.

I get up, wrapping the blanket around myself, putting on my boots and nothing else. I wrap the blanket tightly about myself, and I move toward the open doorway. I step down into the snow on the first step, delighting in the sound of the *crunch* it makes beneath my boot. God, I missed that sound. You never hear that sound in Florida, that delicious *crunch* that marks the beginning of adventures in the mountains, adventures in the great outdoors with the glittering cold and jaw-dropping beauty that will take your breath away.

Everything here is so misty and quiet. I love dreams like this, beautiful dreams that are full of wonder and quiet peace. I don't have too many of them anymore...

The great thing about dreams? I don't remember any of my regrets in them. They're perfectly regret-free.

I take a deep breath then shiver, staring down at my feet standing in the snow. Odd. It feels very real. Very cold. I wiggle my toes inside my boots.

I look down at the snow drifting in through the open doorway, down the two steps outside of the door, and into the yard that sprawls in front of the tall pines, the yard filled with glittering, sparkling folds of snow.

But the perfect snow is broken by jagged tracks descending from the steps down into the yard. I gaze down at the footprints, drawing the blanket even closer, and then...

I stare.

Because the normal, human footprints change. Five feet from the door, the human footprints become...

Well.

Honestly? They look like the prints of a wolf.

I stare at them, my breath coming faster, my breath coming out into the air before me like smoke.

I crouch down on the doorstep, wincing as the cold breeze smarts against the skin of my legs. I stare very carefully at the paw prints.

They're very large. I've seen the prints of large dogs in the sand on the beaches...but these? These prints are far too big. They can't possibly be dog prints, but they *look* like dog prints...just utterly enormous ones.

Like wolf prints.

I stand up again, holding the blanket in tight, cold fingers as I stare at the prints angling away between the distant trees.

Because this is a dream, I'm currently experiencing what only makes sense in a dream: I want to *follow* the tracks.

They're human tracks, the footprints in the snow, but they change into wolf tracks. And I want to see where they're going. Who they came from.

I have a feeling, a very odd feeling, that the paw prints are going to lead me to Kennedy. And, even in this dream, I'm drawn to her. I want to find her.

So I follow the foot prints.

I pull the blanket as close about me as I can, my breath spilling out like smoke into the air as I walk down the steps, the snow crunching beneath the soles of my boots. I walk alongside the paw prints, and my heart is so light, so happy, that even though the snow is deep, and even though it is very, *very* cold, and I'm only wearing boots and a blanket...I'm warm from the inside out.

And even though it's a dream, I can remember Kennedy beneath me, over me. The way her lips curled into a seductive, secretive smile, the way she captured my mouth with hers, the way her skin felt beneath my fingertips. I shiver a little, though this time, not from the cold, as I think of her muscles moving beneath my hands, as I think of what she felt like against me, in me. I reach up, brush my fingers over my hot cheeks, glance down at the prints in the snow.

There was something about her. Something that marked her as so different from anyone I've ever experienced before. *She's not a one-night stand*, I think to myself, following the prints.

I don't want her to be a one-night stand.

I'm beneath the trees now, and I pause, considering that fact. That I don't want to love her and leave her. That there was something about her that drew me to her, that—I'm fairly certain—that there was something about me that drew her in, too. I don't believe in signs or fate or any of that stuff...but then I never imagined that I would have come to a yoga retreat, either.

I turn all of this over in my head gently as I walk beneath the trees now, the moonlight spilling down between the pine branches overhead.

Even though it's night, the moonlight makes it bright as day...

And it's because of the moonlight that I see her.

She's standing ahead of me, between the trees.

Kennedy.

She's perfectly naked, and even though it's quite cold out, I feel the heat of want pass through me, making me shiver, making my breath come out in a long sigh as my eyes follow the contours and muscles of her back, down to her buttocks and her thighs. Her long, red hair is cascading over her back, curling over her shoulders, and she turns in profile now...

But she doesn't see me.

Kennedy lifts her nose to the sky, pursing her beautiful, full lips...and she howls.

The hair on the back of my arms stands up as I watch her howl. She howls, I realize, feeling my heartbeat stir a little faster, exactly like a wolf might.

She sounds, actually, *very* much like a wolf.

And, as I watch her...she changes.

She bends forward, at the waist, her back arching, her head ducking down towards her knees. In one, fluid motion, she presses her hands into the snow, and then, it's all a blur, all of her. I blink, and everything seems to have gone blurry. That's what it looks like.

But it's only a heartbeat that there's a blurred woman in front of me. And then no one woman at all.

A great, white wolf stands in front of me, now, between the trees. She's tall—her shoulders are about the same height as my hips—and, God, she's beautiful. She has the type of raw grace and beauty that takes your breath away. I've never seen anything, I realize, more wild than this gorgeous creature, standing in front of me.

It's a dream, so it makes sense to me, in that moment, that Kennedy would be a wolf. It makes so much sense. What else could she have been, but part wolf? There was such a wildness to her, in the very short time I've known her, such a great sense of ease in the woods. This is who she is, and I know her, standing there, watching the white wolf lift up her nose, watching her throw back her massive, shaggy head...

And the wolf howls.

The howl is not a mournful one, not the sound I'm used to hearing when they play the track of a wolf's howl on a nature documentary or in a movie...no, this sound is different. There are mournful notes to the wolf song, yes. But there's so much more to it. There is a great, wild, feral joy in that long note, a type of music that stirs something primal in my bones. It makes me happy to hear that sound, a raw joy rushing through me, too.

She's beautiful, that wolf, with her head thrown back, her massive white tail dragging in the snow behind her.

But then the wolf stops in her howl, the note trailing away into silence. She brings her head forward, her green eyes, flecked with amber, glittering in the darkness.

She watches as, in the darkness, shadows begin to move.

I lift my head, now, gazing up at the mountain's slope through the tall pine trees. And, racing down the slope toward us, are streaking shadows, loping across the snow.

More wolves.

These wolves are not white. They're gray and brown and black and every mottled combination of those colors. They are all as tall, and they're all different...but none of them are like this great, white wolf. The white wolf, Kennedy, stands a little taller, a little straighter and more noble than the rest. Like an alpha, I realize.

The wolves race down the mountain, and they begin to lope and play around Kennedy. Some play with her, too, racing up to her and licking her snout, shoving their shoulders in affection against her. I'm very familiar with how dogs communicate, and these wolves are communicating in a similar fashion...but a much wilder way.

I watch the wolves play together, Kennedy standing among them. For a long while, they play together, and I am so captivated by their dance that I simply watch them. Then, one by one, they race back up the mountain again, howls lingering behind them, growls and yips filling the clearing.

When all the wolves are gone, Kennedy turns. Her amber-green eyes take me in, her snout lifting.

My breath catches in my throat as she takes one graceful step forward, pressing her enormous paw into the snow.

Then, the wolf is bending forward. She's lengthening, somehow, her body seeming to grow, right in front of my eyes. And then it's Kennedy standing in front of me again, naked, beautiful, glorious Kennedy.

"Trish," she whispers, her brow furrowed. She says nothing else.

For a long moment, we stare at one another. And then I breathe out the breath I didn't even know I was holding.

"You're so beautiful," I tell her, my voice catching. I step forward. I open the blanket, and I wrap it around the both of us, wrapping her in my arms, the blanket draped around our shoulders.

She stays perfectly still while I hold her for the longest time. And then slowly, gently, she raises her hands, pressing her hot palms against the skin of my lower back. She brushes her full mouth against my forehead. She brings her kisses down my nose, covering my nose, my cheeks, my jaw, my chin, my neck.

I melt against her, her warmth cradling me close.

The moonlight washes us in silence, the ghost of the wolf howls traveling away into the mountains, swallowed by the snow.

I had the best sleep of my entire life, but—even then—when I wake up, I'm sore from the bottoms of my feet to the knuckles of my hands.

It was a very...physical evening. And I'm...really not used to that.

I stretch overhead with a wide, cheesy smile, arching my back a little and feeling satisfied when I hear a few "clicks" from my spine as I stretch. I roll over a little, my arm drifting over Kennedy's waist, curling my fingers over the graceful curve of her left hip.

Kennedy is asleep on her stomach, her massive, red curls cascading over her shoulders, the pillow, and my shoulder, too. I rise up on my elbow, and I lean forward a little, brushing my lips to her forehead.

She cracks an eye open, and slowly, lazily, she begins to smile.

"Good morning," she tells me, arching a brow and rolling over onto her side, yawning into the back of her hand.

I glance behind her, at the sky that's just beginning to lighten, and I brush my lips against her mouth this time.

"Good morning," I agree happily.

God, it's been such a long time since it was *truly* a good morning.

"So," says Kennedy, drawing out the word and glancing at me now with a furrowed brow. "Um..." She bites her lip a little, rolling onto her back now. "About last night..." She trails off, waiting, I realize, for me to say something.

"It was *wonderful*," I tell her, breathing the word out and feeling, deep in my gut, exactly how wonderful it was. It was so wonderful, in fact, that I'm having a hard time keeping a straight face, swallowing down the stupid, happy smile that I keep wanting to have.

Because, I realize, dread beginning to creep up my spine...I'm not exactly certain that Kennedy felt the same way.

Because she's staring at me, right now, with a look that doesn't translate as happy. It translates, in fact, as very unhappy indeed. Her brow is furrowed, her full lips are downturned into a frown...

This can't possibly be a good sign.

"Um," I say, because I'm not exactly certain what else *to* say.

A long moment stretches between us before Kennedy lies back down on the bed, pillowing her head beneath her right arm. A smile is beginning to steal across her face. "That's it?" she tells me, wrinkling her nose.

"Um...you were wonderful?" I say, then, because I'm kind of confused. She really *was* amazing...maybe she just needs to be told how good she was. Yeah. That must be it.

"That's *it*?" she persists, her one brow high, a smile more than tugging now at her mouth—she's smiling widely, laughing a little.

When I stare at her again, she laughs even more, covering her face in her hands and laughing into her palms.

"Oh, God, I'm sorry," she says then, rolling over and wrapping me in her arms. She smells so comforting, her scent one I already seem to know by heart, the warmth of her skin against my own something purely delicious. She holds me close, pressing her mouth against mine, kissing me deeply.

"I'm sorry," she repeats, her smile warming me from the inside out. "It's just...funny. That's...really all you remember about last night?"

"Well," I tell her, smiling as I draw a hand through her hair. It's so soft and curly against my fingers, shifting like red satin across my palm—it's exactly what I thought it would feel like. "I *did* have an interesting dream," I tell her then.

"Oh," she says, her eyes sparkling. "What did you dream?"

"There's probably something Freudian going on," I tell her, raising one of my brows now, "but I dreamed you became a wolf."

Kennedy was in the middle of working a trail of kisses down my neck, but she stops now, her lips pressed against my skin.

I sit up a little, because there's something nagging at me...

I glance down, and bite my lip.

I'm wearing my boots.

I know, absolutely, that I did not take Kennedy to bed while wearing boots.

I glance to the glass wall...

The sun is rising, but because of the mountains, it's not bright daylight yet. But I don't need bright daylight to see the fact that there are wolf tracks outside in the yard. Wolf tracks, and human tracks, both.

Kennedy trails a hot finger down my back, making me shiver. "Was it a good dream?" she asks me, her low voice a growl. I glance down at her, down at her sparkling eyes and her smiling mouth.

I take a deep breath, lie back down, pillowing my head on her shoulder as she draws me close.

"A...very good one," I say tentatively, considering things.

We stay very quiet for a long moment as my world view is neatly exploded, and then reordered, as Kennedy traces her fingers up and down my arm, her breathing steady as she brushes her lips to the top of my head.

"Funny how everything can change in a night," she says quietly then.

I reach up, cupping my hand at her jaw and chin, pressing my fingers gently through her hair as I rise on an elbow, staring down at this raw, fierce, gorgeous creature.

"Yeah," I tell her. "Funny, that."

And, without a single regret in the world, I lean down, and I kiss Kennedy fiercely, the old me and the new me becoming, in that moment, one.

The sun rises over the Rocky Mountains, shining down on the wolf tracks behind the retreat center. There might be a logical explanation. It might just have been a very good dream.

But, no matter what or who she is, Kennedy's kiss is bright and real and the most wonderful thing I've experienced since I can remember.

"So," she tells me, her mouth twitching upward at the corners as she tries to maintain a serious expression. "Are you ready for your morning yoga session?"

"Oh, God," I mutter, chuckling as I hide my face in her shoulder, feeling my cheeks color. "I...actually have something to tell you..."

"Don't worry," says Kennedy softly, gently,

working her fingers into my hair and kissing me fiercely. "There's a first time for everything," she promises me. "Or, you know..." she tells me, one brow up, "we could postpone the yoga..." She trails her fingers down my bare stomach, causing me to shiver. "Just for a little while..."

Kennedy pulls me down on top of her with a low, throaty chuckle then, and I pull off my boots with a laugh.

After all, you only live once.

-- Wolf Queen --

"So, this is a little weird..."

I look up from my desk and stare at my boss Douglas in surprise. Douglas isn't the type of man who I would ever expect to call something "weird." To be honest, I assume the man eats Weird Flakes for breakfast—and that's an assumption that I harbor with a great amount of affection. Douglas has made an art of weird.

Today he's staring down at me with his cockatiel Rudy perched on his bald head. The bird, squawking angrily, keeps slipping over Douglas' forehead because of said baldness. Not a lot of traction there.

"Hit me with your best shot, Doug," I say, leaning back in my faux leather chair and smiling widely as I spread my hands. "If you think something's weird, it's got to be really, *really* weird."

"Oh, it is," he tells me with a grimace, helping Rudy off of his head and onto his brightly colored shoulder. The cockatiel hunkers down on the floral-printed fabric of Doug's Hawaiian shirt, his feathers fluffed. Then Doug clears his throat, running a hand over his bald pate, which he always does whenever he's nervous.

"So, Amber," he says, drawing out my name as he gives me a funny look, one brow raised. "Did you know that Howl was sold?" he asks me.

"Howl? As in the nightclub?" I blink at him as he nods.

I shrug a little, perplexed. Howl is a nightclub down the street from us here in Lakeview, one of the gayer, more colorful and all-around wonderful neighborhoods in Chicago. I've never stepped foot over the threshold of Howl, and not just because nightclubs aren't my scene. I passed Howl plenty of times on my way home, and the loud Top 40 music that poured out of those doors told me all I needed to know: that the place was probably full of straight, high, drunk college kids tossing back tequila shots and margaritas while sloppily hitting on one another. Thanks, but no thanks.

"Well, *that's* not the weird part," says Doug, his tone becoming a little wheedling as his smile grows. "We want to cover the club's grand reopening for the paper, of course."

"Do we?" I groan, folding over and hitting my head softly on the desk.

"Amber Clancy," says Doug, his southern accent becoming more pronounced as he juts out one of his hips and puts his hands on both of them, tut-tutting like a chastising mother hen. "Do I pay you to sit around here and look pretty?"

I chuckle a little and swat at his arm. "Hey, that's why I earn the big bucks, right?" I tell him with a wink. And then I groan again, shaking my head, my curly black hair sweeping over my shoulders. "So, are you saying you want *me* to go down and interview the new owner or something?" I ask him, as I fold my arms in front of me. "Get the big scoop on why *anyone* would want to buy the only straight club within ten blocks of the gayest neighborhood in Chicago?"

"Well, something like that—but maybe phrase it a little more nicely," says Doug, removing the pink boa that was draped around his neck; Rudy had begun to groom its feathers with his beak. Smiling, Douglas slings the boa around my neck, instead.

"But," he tells me evenly, biting at his lip as he adjusts the boa to his satisfaction, "the *really* weird thing is that they *asked* for you, specifically, to come interview the new owner for this article. You!"

"Wow, you're doing wonders for my self-esteem," I smirk, tossing my cell phone and an old-fashioned yellow legal pad into my big purse, along with a handful of pens. I pin Doug in my sights and snort as I unwind his sacred boa (he always wears it when he's editing) and set it reverently on the desk. "Is it really so hard for you to believe that people actually read *Proud and Windy*—and that they might love my articles?"

"Honey, none of us has any illusions about our precious little paper here," says Doug, shaking his head with a soft chuckle. "We all know that people read *Proud and Windy*," Doug tells me, patting my shoulder, "for the *Personals* section. But, hey, the sponsors keep buying ads, and we keep on publishing, so hell... It keeps us in peanut butter, right?"

"Right," I tell him, my lips twitching into a grin despite my resolve to keep teasing him. "Lots of peanut butter. Because it's all I can afford to eat on this salary," I say, raising an eyebrow.

Doug lifts his hands in an "I surrender" position and shakes his head. "Howl is paying for a full-page ad in next week's paper, and they've pledged to keep putting that ad in, weekly, for the indefinite future. So if they want you to come down and do an article on the reopening, let's give the people—"

"What they want," I finish, reciting the unofficial motto of *Proud and Windy*. Which is, admittedly, a terrible name for a free gay newspaper, but the rag's been around since the eighties, and we might lose readers if we changed the name now.

Still, Douglas is right: we're under no delusions that we're publishing *The New York Times*.

Cockatiel Rudy chooses that moment to poop on Doug's shoulder and flap away, cackling to himself merrily, as if he is very aware of what he's just done—and he finds it hilarious. He lands on Doug's very, *very* messy desk, strewn with wrappers, papers and past newspapers, sending several flying into the air.

"You know, it's a great sign of affection for a bird to poop on you," says Doug with a wink and a smile, taking one of my tissues from my tissue box and wiping off his shirt with a sigh. "It means they trust and are comfortable with you."

"Just don't let him get that comfortable with me," I tell Doug, eyeing the gray-and-yellow bird, who is currently grooming his feathers.

"All right," I say then, patting my purse to make certain everything I need is in it before slinging it onto my shoulder. I glance at the clock. "After this, I'm off, okay?" I tell Doug, my head to the side. He glances at me, brows up, and I gesture to the clock. "It's almost four, anyway. I'll head down to Howl, get the scoop on the opening. Then there's a big date for me tonight."

Doug stares at me, his mouth open, his eyes wide. He holds his silence for a comically long moment, and then he splutters: "*Seriously?*"

"Again with the self-esteem!" I groan. "You're a jerk, Doug," I tell him with a little smile.

"No, no, I was just happy for you. That's all," he says, then notices my face. "Well, crap. You *were* joking," he sighs. "You're *not* going on a date tonight, Amber?" he asks me, a little too hopefully.

I echo his sigh and shake my head, making my voice sound a little more cheerful than I feel as I toss my hair over my shoulder. "Hey, doing dishes *is* a date for me. Have you seen my sink? Those dirty dishes are going to become sentient soon," I quip, but my good mood is starting to dissolve.

God, if my *boss* thinks it's a crazy notion for me to be going out on a date...what does that say for me? That I'm doomed to be single for the rest of my life?

I really, *really* hope not.

"Work on your motivational speeches," I tell Doug gently, then wink at him again—there's no hard feelings. "I'll see you tomorrow."

"Knock 'em dead, kid," says Doug, like he does every afternoon, running his hand over his bald head again and giving me his genuine, encouraging smile.

"Always," I promise, and then I'm out the door of Chicago's tiniest office space. Not that we need a bigger place. Most days, it's just me, Doug, Rudy (who *is* on the payroll for *Proud and Windy* but gets paid, appropriately, in birdseed), and Latoya, the glue who holds us all together. Without her, the magazine would look *terrible*, but thanks to her graphic design and formatting abilities (and the millions of other little tasks she does), *Proud and Windy* is something to be...well, *proud* of.

That's one of our other unofficial mottoes. And...you don't want to know the others—trust me!

As I press the button, waiting for the elevator to creep its slow, ancient way up to our nineteenth floor, I

169

lean against the wall and breathe out with a sigh, pressing my right palm against the cool marble to ground and steady myself. It doesn't work.

I love Doug: he's my boss, yes, but he's a friend I really love and respect. I know he didn't mean anything by his comments; he was just teasing like he always does... But for some reason, it hurt a little today.

I sigh again and stare up at the ceiling, biting my lip. It's a little juvenile, admittedly, but my very first reaction is defensiveness. I mean, I *could* go out tonight and get a girl. I *know* I could. I hold tightly to my purse strap and take a deep breath.

I could get a girl, sure.

But that girl wouldn't be *her*.

It's been seven years since I last saw her.

I'm angry as I press the elevator button again—and again, fully realizing that this doesn't make the elevator come any faster. I dash away the single tear that crept out of my eye and leaked down my cheek. *Seven years.* You'd think I could move on in *seven years*. That's...that's forever, really. And, God knows, as well-intentioned Doug likes to remind me, I'm not getting any younger. (Though why, at the age of twenty-five, I'm suddenly hitting an expiration date, I'll never know.) Doug tells me that I need to get out there, get into the dating scene, sow my wild oats.

But I don't.

So here's my terrible secret: I have been on approximately ten dates since I moved to Chicago. A couple of those dates were with the same women, but we didn't really hit it off in the end. Half a dozen times, I went down to T's Bar, one of the bigger lesbian bars in Chicago, and picked up a lady for the night, but those outings (ha!) were few and far between.

When my sister Meg calls me up and pesters me about why I don't have a girlfriend, I tell her it's because my job is keeping me too busy. Which is an outright lie, but I don't want Meg to worry so much about me. Though she worries, anyway. She got the worry gene in the family.

So I've been in Chicago for seven years. Ten dates and a couple of flings in seven years. The math is staggeringly bad, and though Doug may have been teasing...he's kind of right. It *would* be pretty out of the ordinary for me to be going on a date tonight.

Not because I *can't* get a girl, I think, as defensiveness prickles my skin.

But because I don't *want* a random woman...

I want...her.

Stevie.

I pale as I allow myself to think of her perfect name. I close my eyes, my palm still pressed against the marble of the wall, now warming to my touch. I think about her for only a moment...

Well, I only ever allow myself to think about her, *really* think about her, for a moment.

Any longer, and the heartache is too strong, too lancing for me to handle.

The elevator finally arrives, *dinging* open. I take a deep breath, shake my head and step into it, hitting the bottom floor button. I then proceed to age about fifty years waiting for the elevator to reach to the main floor. I look at my reflection, very carefully *not* thinking about anything but how I look today (a total distraction, but, hey—it's working).

I have shoulder-length black hair that curls so tightly that sometimes, when it's humid out, I look like I'm wearing a black mop on my head. Today, blessedly, it's not *too* humid, and my hair doesn't look half bad. I wear big, geeky glasses, but I think they look kind of cute. My outfit of choice normally consists of—as it does today—a cardigan and a skirt and tights. But lately, I've been feeling kind of frumpy, wearing the same cardigans over and over again.

Yeah. That's it. That's what's gotten me down. Not Doug's assertion that it would be crazy for me to be going out on a date.

Not thoughts about Stevie.

I'm kind of mopey as I walk the few blocks from the office to Howl, though I'm trying not to show it. It really *is* a beautiful day, the kind of June afternoon that you usually can only pine for in Chicago. June is typically as hot as the surface of the sun around here. But it's not swelteringly hot, and the breeze from Lake Michigan is something you feel dancing over your skin, even this far into the city.

I can smell water in the air... Maybe there'll be a rainstorm tonight.

I put on my game face as I approach Howl. The nightclub has always looked pretty nondescript to me, but as I round the block, I'm surprised to see that they're putting in a new electric sign over the front door, removing the one that was probably installed in the eighties, with about seventy-five percent of the light bulbs inside of it burned out for years.

The new sign isn't just a replacement but a revision. It looks like they're changing the club's name to—I peer closer—*Wolf Queen*.

There's a woman perched precariously on a tall ladder with a power drill, drilling a few more screws into the metal strip below the sign. She glances down at me in surprise when I walk directly beneath the ladder, heading toward the staircase leading down to the club's door. I notice in passing that the woman is wearing a business suit and really doesn't look like she belongs on ladders or wielding power tools—but then again, looks can be deceiving.

"Walking right under a ladder?" she asks me, waving the drill. "Don't you believe in bad luck?"

I glance up at her and shrug a little. "Luck? No, not really," I say, with a small, rueful smile. "Hey, do you know where I can find the owner of the club? I'm Amber Clancy. I'm with *Proud and Windy*," I say, my smile broadening. It always helps, I've found, to deliver the name of our newspaper with a smile; otherwise people ask for the name again, and you have to pronounce it a little more clearly, and then everyone ends up feeling awkward.

I clear my throat and lift my chin. "I'm here to interview him about the reopening of the club?"

The woman begins to climb down the ladder, and it's then that I realize she's wearing high heels, impressively tall ones. She manages the steps quite well. As she descends, she raises a single brow, and when she's standing on the sidewalk beside me, she's smiling, too, as she sets the power drill in an open tool bag on the ground, brushing her hands together.

"Her," she corrects me then, tilting her head to the side.

I lift an eyebrow.

"This club was just bought by—" the woman begins, but she gets cut off.

"Jessica?" comes a voice from inside the club, drifting up the concrete stairs from the a door below ground level. The voice is warm and low, a woman's voice, so pleasant and undeniably sexy in its lower register that I actually feel the hairs on the back of my neck stand up...

But they're standing up for another reason, too. I shiver.

For a weird, electric moment...time stands still.

"Are you done with the sign?" the voice asks, coming closer, the woman who possesses it climbing those concrete steps toward us. "Because we may have used the wrong screws on the small corner piece, and I think they installed it incorrectly, so I'm going to give the contractor a call—"

I'm standing, yes, but it suddenly feels like the world is falling away from me. Because... It's odd, impossible, but...

But I *know* that voice.

I take a deep breath, my heartbeat thundering inside of me as I try to explain away what I'm hearing. I know, logically, that it can't be her. And yet, it sounded just like...

The woman continues to walk up the concrete steps from the below-ground club. She's fallen silent now, as she puts one foot in front of the other. Finally, she stops on the landing. We're standing only about three feet apart, and when I look at her, the world screeches to a halt. I'm sure that time still moves around the both of us, flowing like a river, but it feels as if the earth itself has stopped turning.

Because somehow, it's her.

"Stevie," I whisper, the word falling from my lips.

It's been seven years. Seven long, excruciating years, and I *know* that I've changed, but Stephanie Whitmore has somehow, maddeningly, remained the same. Maybe she's a little different: her long, shining black hair isn't loose around her shoulders anymore; it's been drawn up into a high ponytail that spills over her shoulder like a night full of stars. She's more muscled than she used to be, a fact that's quite noticeable because she's wearing an athletic tank top and hip-hugging jeans, jeans so tight that I can see the muscles outlined beneath them. She must have taken up working out after she...

After she didn't show up that night.

I feel dizzy. This can't be real... But I know it's real. There are so many memories vying for attention in my head, and while I try to and mostly succeed in pushing them away every other day, I can't seem to do that now, not when I'm standing directly in front of the woman who shattered my heart.

What can I possibly say to her?

But I don't have to say anything. Because the iPad that Stevie was holding in her fingers starts to slip from her hands. She's staring at me, her full lips parted. And somewhere deep inside of me, I'm glad that she's just as shocked to see me as I am to see her. Her high cheekbones still draw my eyes, just like they used to, and those gorgeous, sculpted brows still pull my gaze. She was beautiful seven years ago in a gangly, teenage way, but she's matured into a woman so magnetic that she...

She takes my breath away.

The iPad is out of her grasp now, falling to the ground, and neither of us is moving to stop it. But then the woman who'd been on the ladder—Jessica, I think her name is—catches the iPad before it crashes onto the unforgiving concrete.

Jessica holds the computer to her chest, and then she clears her throat, glancing from me to Stevie, back to me again, with one brow raised, her mouth pursed.

And that's what breaks the spell. The two of us wake up, shaking ourselves as if from out of a trance. I fold my arms in front of me, but Stevie lifts a hand, as if she's trying to soothe a frightened animal.

"Hello," Stevie whispers then, the word low and soft, as if she's afraid to give voice to it, as if she doesn't know what to say. She coughs, says, "Hello, Amber," as her hand drops back down to her side.

I stare at her like I'm seeing a ghost. I almost am.

Because seven years have disappeared, just like that. I'm back in Kankakee in the blink of an eye, waiting that night...

Waiting for her.

"Look," says Jessica, taking a step backward, holding up the iPad as she shrugs a little sheepishly. "I'm just going to...uh...head back inside." She picks up the bag of tools and turns away from us.

Stevie licks her lips, blinks, shakes her head. "Will you please come in, Amber?" she asks me quietly, gesturing behind her toward the steps that lead down to the nightclub's entrance. "Can I offer you a drink?" she asks me soberly, holding my gaze with her unwavering brown eyes, a brown that's so deep and dark and absolute that they're almost black.

I used to be able to get lost in those eyes. But I can't anymore. I feel like I'm falling to pieces as I stare at Stevie, as I find myself unable to say anything to her. And, God, I want to say so much.

In a single heartbeat, I run the gamut of emotions: shock, blistering anger, deep and total heartache—and, at the end of them all, the one I'm most ashamed of...

A flicker of hope opens its wings deep inside of my belly.

"Please, Amber, come inside," says Stevie, taking a step forward, holding her hand out to me. That hand that traced its palm over my heart. That hand that I held so tightly I thought I'd never let it go.

I don't take her hand, can't, and after a long, silent moment, she drops it beside her thigh again. There's a haunted, hunted look in her eyes, and I'm fairly certain I'm not the only one time-traveling right now, going back seven years, to a warm, humid night full of possibility...

That night that was supposed to change both of our lives forever.

And my life did change—irrevocably.

Just...not in the way it was supposed to.

I'd just turned eighteen, which was one of the most exciting things that had ever happened to me. I don't know if you've ever been to Kankakee, Illinois, but it's not a tremendously nice place. Oh, it's all right, I guess, for what it is. It's this smallish town outside of Chicago that's bordered by a lot of farmland, and it's full of kids wanting to escape. There is, sadly, a ton of crime in Kankakee, because there *are* all of these kids wanting to escape... To put things into perspective, Letterman donated two gazebos to the town in '99 because it was rated the *worst* metropolitan area in the country to live. That's my city!

So everyone either wanted to get away or were content to live there indefinitely...

But me? Well, I'd worked out a plan to get the hell out of Dodge. I didn't love my town, and I didn't want to stay there. I was going to move to Chicago come hell or high water.

But that wasn't the best part.

The best part was that Stevie was coming *with* me.

Stevie? Stevie was my entire *world*. The reason I got up in the morning, and the reason that my life was good and not terrible, like it should have been. I lived in a small, rundown trailer park on the outskirts of Kankakee, which was just as rotten as it sounds. And it wasn't that I was better than anyone there—because I wasn't. It's that I had big dreams, and I wanted more than anything to make them a reality, and I knew that my dreams weren't going to come true in Kankakee.

I wanted to be a writer, the kind of writer whose articles you read in *Time* or *Vanity Fair* or, really, any publication bigger than my school newspaper. My English teacher told me I had talent, and I wanted to see where it could take me. With my drive and determination, I hoped I could make something of myself.

So, yes, I wanted to move to the "big city," as cliché as that sounds, for a million reasons, like being able to get a good job doing what I love. But the biggest reason I wanted to make a home for myself in Chicago—the most *important* reason—was one I'd been hiding for a very long time.

And it was this: moving to Chicago would mean that I could be free to be myself. Because I was gay in a town that didn't exactly welcome gay people.

And I was keeping it a secret.

Maybe you've hidden part of yourself from others like I have... Maybe you know what it's like, that searing ache, deep in your chest, to constantly be afraid of being caught, to constantly be afraid that somehow, just by looking at you...they'll *know*. I lived with that terror every single day, trying to act so *straight* in a world that would ruin me, if it knew who I really was.

My mother was dead, and my father was doing the best he could to raise me and my sister Meg on minimum wage, working for the gravel plant. And he was a good man, and he loved me very much...but I was under no misconceptions. I knew that the moment he found out I was gay, no matter how much he loved me, it just wasn't going to be something he'd be able to stomach or even understand. I knew he was going to throw me out into the streets. Being gay to him was something dirty, something only the lowest of the low were, and if I was gay, that would mean that I was, by association, bad, filthy, evil. And I would be asked to leave his presence, and that of my sister, forcibly.

I couldn't imagine leaving my home like that, and I wanted to beat him to the punch, if I possibly could. I wanted to leave home under my *own* power, not be thrown out of it, and I, above all else, desperately wanted the freedom to be myself.

Chicago, like a far-off Emerald City, glittered full of raw possibility and hope. Chicago, which had a *Pride* parade. A parade that *celebrated* being gay, rather than condemning it. I could hardly believe it sometimes, because it seemed, living in Kankakee, that Stevie and I were the only gay people in the world.

But in Chicago? I knew there were other people like us, maybe a whole *lot* of other people like us...and I hungered for that community desperately.

I'd met Stevie when we were just kids. She'd moved to Kankakee from Anchorage when we were both about ten years old. Anchorage was, to my mind, a whole world away, and Stevie was exotic and cool to me because of that.

But there was so much more to Stephanie Whitmore than where she'd come from.

Even when I was ten, I knew that Stevie was the one for me. Yes, I knew that, bone deep, when I was that young. I knew it like I knew that my favorite ice cream flavor was strawberry, like I knew that you had to be careful swimming in the Kankakee River in the spring, because it drowned kids all the time.

I knew it like I knew nothing else. I *knew* that Stevie was the one.

And the first time I knew that was the very first moment I saw her.

It was a late August afternoon, and I'd just come back from swimming in the river. I was dripping wet when I'd started home, barefoot and wringing my hair out on the path, but the walk back to the trailer park had dried me almost completely. It was hotter than hell, and I was contemplating heading right back to the river (I was already sweaty again, and I'd gone for a swim to remedy that) when I saw her on the edge of the park.

She was lying on a big, flat rock in front of her trailer, one of the older trailers that was in greater disrepair than the others.

She was sunning herself on that rock, her long, black hair fanned out around her face, her face with its high cheekbones and effortlessly graceful lines already so beautiful. She had long black lashes that rested gently along her tan cheeks, quivering as she dreamed—because she was fast asleep. She was lean and lanky; I knew just from looking at her that she was going to be tall. She had one leg up, crossed over her knee, and her hands were pillowed behind her head, and she looked perfectly relaxed. Even in sleep, there was this smile on her face. She looked so peaceful...so...*happy*.

I was pretty sure that I *never* looked peaceful, not even in my sleep, so to see someone who was so effortlessly content... Well, something happened inside of me. Something that unfurled, deep within, that drew me to her like a moth to a flame, pulling me forward. I wanted, desperately, whatever it was that she had inside of her, that could make someone who looked like she was in a situation very much like my own feel...happy.

I would later find out that her life was actually much worse than my own. Her parents had lost their jobs in Anchorage, and Stevie's grandparents had taken in Stevie and Carl, her brother, while the parents looked for jobs. Or, at least, that's what Stevie told me, and at the time, I believed it. Probably her parents had skipped town on the kids, or been killed, but I never learned the true story. Her grandparents were quiet and kept to themselves, and I never saw them much, but it seemed to me like Stevie's relationship with them was strained. And her brother was a little jerk, constantly getting expelled, vandalizing things from a very young age, and eventually trying to set fire to the school, for which he was caught and expelled.

So the thing was, Stevie *didn't* have a good home life like I did. She had a terrible one.

But you could never have known that, that late August afternoon, the sun filtering down through the trees on the edge of the trailer park, covering her in a glow of gold, her hair changing colors like a raven's wing, midnight black one moment and then a deep, burnished blue. My eyes followed the shifting patterns of the light over her hair, the shadows of the leaves on her skin.

We were both ten years old, and—in that moment—my heart skipped a beat for the very first time.

I'd stopped on the path, stopped and paused as I was awestruck by the sight of this new girl. But when I took a step forward to continue on my way toward my own trailer—I couldn't bring myself to disturb her; she looked too peaceful—my foot fell on a small stick, and it broke beneath my weight. It was a relatively soft *snap*, and the sound of the highway right beyond this perimeter of trees should have drowned it out, but she heard me, anyway. She heard me, and her eyes flicked open and took me in as she sat up on her elbow, her lips lifting into a soft smile as she gazed at me.

When our eyes connected... I'll never forget that feeling. Her eyes were so dark in her softly tanned face, so dark they were almost black, a depth to the brown of them that reminded me of the forest deep beneath the trees, in the shadow of tall pines. Her eyes were like the stillness of an overgrown wood, calm yet somehow wild, free.

I'd only been in the woods once. There weren't many forests around Kankakee, with the flat land full of cornfields surrounding us, and I hadn't been out of Kankakee much. But once, we'd gone to the Arboretum near Chicago. This was before my mother died. I didn't know my mother was dying at the time (I was really little), and I wandered that big park like a wild hooligan, a huge smile on my face the entire day, because beneath those trees, I had found something that I'd never known I craved my whole life.

It was the first time I'd felt peace.

I felt that exact same peace, the same deepness of contentment, as I locked eyes with this girl. Her long black hair was draped around her shoulders, and I don't know why I thought it, but I did:

Even though she was smiling at me, even though she looked perfectly relaxed...she looked...

Well, she looked *wild* to me.

And I liked that. I liked that very much.

"Hello," she told me, in the softest voice imaginable, soft and low like a bumblebee's hum. Her lips turned up more at the corners, and then she was genuinely smiling as she sat up fully, leaning forward, leaning toward me. She pinned me to the spot with that intense, brown-eyed gaze, and I found myself clearing my throat.

"Hello," I told her, shuffling my feet beneath me, because I was suddenly shy. She'd caught me watching her.

There was a long moment of silence between us as she took me in, as we stared at one another.

"My name is Stevie," she finally said, like she was telling me a secret. She lifted her chin, her dark eyes flashing triumphantly as she got up from the rock, brushing off the butt of her jeans with tan hands. She raised an eyebrow at me, her grin widening. She took a few quick steps forward and jutted out her hand. "What's your name?"

"Amber," I told her, taking her hand gingerly and shaking it, just like the grownups did. I'd never shaken the hand of another child before. Stevie's palm was very warm and just a little sweaty, and she shook my hand with a great deal of strength. I liked that, too.

"Well, Amber," she said, not letting go of my hand but pulling me forward and wrapping her arms around me. She nestled her nose in my hair, a little bit like a dog would, inhaling deeply. I stiffened in her embrace, because I was suddenly worried that I still smelled like stale sweat, like I'd done before taking the swim in the river, but this strange girl pillowed her cheek on my shoulder with a happy sigh.

"I wanted a friend," she murmured wistfully, drawing back and batting her long lashes at me as her mouth turned up at the corners. "Will you be my friend?" she asked me then, taking a step back, holding tightly to my shoulders with her strong, small hands.

I took a deep breath. "I've...I've been wanting a friend, too," I said, surprising no one more than myself. Had I really just told this complete stranger the truth, the truth that I normally kept hidden in my heart, that I was desperately lonely?

Sure, I had my little sister, and I loved her, and she was my friend, but I wanted something...more. I wanted the type of friend that I saw on Disney movies, the kind of inseparable friend you go on adventures with, discover the world with, connected together forever through the journeys you've undergone and all you've shared together.

"Well, then...let's be friends," Stevie told me simply, her lips twitching into a secret smile as she drew me close again. She had her nose buried in my hair for a second time, her arms wrapped tightly around me, holding me as close as a secret.

As we stood there beneath the branches of that lone tree on the edge of our trailer park, as we embraced tightly, and as Stevie chuckled, the cicadas singing around us...I knew. I was only ten years old, and I'd experienced little of life at that point, but I still knew, at that moment, that Stevie was going to be the most important person in my life—forever.

And I was right.

We were inseparable as we grew older, the two of us constantly together, every moment of every day. We knew each other instinctively, knew what the other was thinking, how the other would react, what the other was going to say. And if Stevie was a little different from the other girls at school, I chalked that up to her being better than them. I wasn't better, but I knew Stevie was.

Stevie was better than everyone.

When I was sixteen years old, the feelings that had been unfurling deep inside of me suddenly had no place else to go. I had felt attraction for Stevie constantly since I'd hit puberty, and the attraction was growing, strong and silent and aching. I couldn't contain the wishes and wants anymore, could no longer squish them down, shoving them into boxes and locking doors in my own mind and heart.

I knew that I was in love with Stevie.

I'd known I loved her from the very first moment I saw her, but I didn't understand what that meant. At sixteen, though, with a sixteen-year-old's perception of the world, with hormones raging through me, I understood, and deeply, exactly what this could do to the two of us if I told her how I felt.

The hardest part of all of this was that there had been no indication that Stevie was like me. I was attracted to girls, and that made me a lesbian. I knew the word *lesbian* because of how the kids threw it around at school—always as an insult—and I knew that word related to me. I was a lesbian because I liked girls...but what was Stevie?

It was true: Stevie had never been on a date with a guy, had never made out with any of the guys at school, had never really been *seen* with any of the guys, and she certainly didn't seem to like any of them. But I wasn't sure what that meant. Stevie was her own person, and she was a little quirky. Her lack of interest in boys didn't mean she was gay.

Stevie was, and had always been, unique. She was wild, and everyone knew that. Not in the binge-drinking, partying way that a lot of the other kids around Kankakee were wild.

No. Stevie was really and truly *wild*.

She would wake up in the middle of the night, sneak past her sleeping grandparents and her evil little brother snoring in his little bed, and she would close the door of her trailer silently behind her, sprinting across the trailer park to my window. She would knock on it gently, tapping three times so I knew it was her, and I'd wake right up, or maybe I'd already been awake, waiting for her, and I'd get out of bed, my heart racing as I snuck out of my trailer. My dad was a fast sleeper, and my kid sister slept like the dead, so it wasn't really a James Bond mission or anything, but I'd feel the thrill of it all the same.

Because once out of the trailer, I'd fall into Stevie's arms, embracing her in the moonlight, our arms wrapping around each other so tightly that it felt, in those moments, like we would never let go.

Stevie wasn't afraid of *anything*. She'd take my hand, and the two of us would run together, run until we couldn't breathe anymore, and then keep running, taking in great big lungfuls of air as we laughed, sprinting across the train tracks until we were actually outside of Kankakee, the wind rustling through the corn stalks, a whole wash of stars and the moon overhead, lighting the way.

And then we'd keep running, running through the cow fields, running together hand in hand until we reached the bend in the river. The bend in the river that was *ours*.

It wasn't really ours, obviously. We didn't own that spot of land; a cow farmer did. But we'd claimed it, anyway. We'd rigged up a sort of house out of debris that had conveniently landed close by from one of the last big tornadoes: a swatch of siding that had probably been taken from somebody's trailer, hurled apart and broken into manageable bits by the storm. This siding was about eight feet by eight feet, and it was enough of a wall for us, so that's what we used it for.

We'd leaned the bit of siding against the only tree at that bend in the river, a scraggly, stunted thing that somehow survived the terrible storms and tornadoes to keep standing. After laying the siding against it, we'd grabbed some other boards from Dumpsters in Kankakee and a sort of garbage pit that had been set up in one of the fields, and we had rigged up a second side of this shack, the third side being the trunk of the tree and the fourth being the wide open air. It was jury-rigged and would probably fall over during the next big windstorm, but for that entire month, the little shed remained steady, in place.

Stevie pulled me into the makeshift shed gently, tugging at my arm with her smile curving upward like a crescent moon, and it was there that we kissed each other in the moonlight filtering down through the branches, there that we tasted every inch of one another's skin. And I knew, in those moments, that there was nothing more that I wanted than to be with her.

To be with her. In Chicago. Just the two of us, completely free.

"We can go together," I'd tell her, over and over. And though Stevie was wild and adventurous in all other ways...for some reason that I didn't understand, she was reticent about this. She didn't want to go, and I just couldn't understand that.

"But *why* don't you want to go?" I'd ask her in exasperation, my heart aching inside of me as I gripped her arms, holding her gaze. "We...we could be *together*, Stevie, and we could be *out*," I told her, like it was the most obvious thing in the world. "We wouldn't have to hide anymore, and then we could build our lives together, and we'd be *happy*, Stevie," I'd tell her, holding her hands tightly in my own, as if I could squeeze the knowledge into her.

"But we *are* happy, Amber," she told me gently, searching my eyes. And then her jaw clenched, and she sighed, looking away. "You know I can't leave my family," she said, her words so soft that I would have to strain to hear them.

And that's something I couldn't make sense of. Because I had a happy family life, for the most part, but Stevie's home life was awful. Her grandparents hated her and her brother, her brother hated her, and the whole lot of them were so contentious and miserable. Stevie was the only one who held them together with her kindness, her big heart... She was the glue that made their lives somewhat bearable.

But that was, in my mind, a *better* reason to leave them. They used her; they were horrific to her. There was, in my mind, absolutely no reason to stay.

Now I know that family matters aren't so simple. But I was sixteen years old then, about to turn seventeen. I didn't fully understand that some acts can be irreversible, and that people can leave your life forever because of your words or your actions. I didn't understand because, in a lot of ways, I was still a kid.

But I think Stevie knew. And she wasn't ready to face that yet.

Stevie told me that she couldn't leave her family...and though she was gentle and kind in her telling me no, it was an absolute, immovable no. There was seemingly no way to convince her to change her mind, and I did my best to respect that.

I would occasionally bring the subject up, but I tried not to press her. Every day at home, I was worried. Worried that, somehow, my father would find out about Stevie and me. Worried that, somehow, he would notice that I didn't bring guys around, not like the other girls in the trailer park, that he would see through my weak excuses of "too much schoolwork!" and "too busy with after-school activities!" But he worked through his shifts and came home exhausted, so he didn't notice much. Still, I worried. I was afraid.

But, finally, when we were in our senior year...everything changed.

Stevie and I were sitting at the bend in our river. Many months ago, another tornado had ripped through and taken the bits of siding that we kept propping up against the tree, so we no longer had our little shack. It was a cold, rainy March night, but we were bundled up together, wrapped so tightly in one another that I didn't know where I ended and she began, and I loved it that way. I loved it when we were wrapped up so tightly that we were, essentially, inseparable.

"Let's go," she whispered in my ear, her arms holding me close.

The rain was pouring down steadily, and it pockmarked the surface of the river so that it looked like the surface of the moon. I remember that, remember it as clearly as if it just happened. Because my heart began to rise within me.

I knew she wasn't talking about heading home.

I knew she was talking about Chicago.

"Really?" I asked her, looking back. Her jaw was clenched, and she was staring out at the river, but then she fixed her beautiful brown eyes on me, and she nodded once, twice.

"I want to go with you," she said, squeezing me gently. "There's nothing for me here anymore. I know that now," she whispered. "This isn't my home," she told me, gazing deeply into my eyes. "*You* are."

Though I could feel her sincerity—and it thrilled me, utterly—there was something wrong in all of this, something just the tiniest bit off... Unlike me, Stevie never talked in this way about her family, about Kankakee. Why now? Why today? What had happened?

I looked at her, straightening, holding her gaze. My heart was soaring inside of me—she'd just called me, us, her *home*. But...

"What's wrong?" I asked her quietly.

She looked away, her jaw clenching even tighter. "Things are all right," she said, the words sounding forced, coming out between her clenched teeth in a growl. She didn't sound as if she were telling me the whole truth, but she kept talking. "I...I just don't belong here anymore. I don't think I belonged here from the start. But I'm glad that I came here. That I met you," she whispered, brushing her warm, full lips over the end of my nose in a chaste kiss... And then she captured my mouth with her own, and she kissed me with enough passion to make me forget what she'd just said about her family...

But I didn't let it go. I backed away, held her gaze again.

"Stevie, what's *wrong*?" I asked, my heart beating faster in my chest.

But she wouldn't tell me.

I soon forgot the details of that night, forgot everything except for Stevie telling me that we were going to go to Chicago together. My greatest dream was coming true. Soon, we'd be free to be together openly. Soon, I wouldn't have to hide who I was. It was exhilarating, that thought, though the exhilaration came from naivete. Still, those were some of the happiest months of my life.

Because we had to plan for months to get it all right. And this is what we'd come up with: the night of our high school graduation, we would both be eighteen (Stevie had turned a few months earlier, and me a few weeks earlier), so we could go and do anything we wanted—as long as we could afford it. We were going to take that freedom and run with it, run away.

We'd been saving up for months from our jobs as gas station attendants, and we'd already bought one-way Greyhound tickets to Chicago. We were going to ride into the city. We had enough money for a motel that first night, then three months' worth of rent each for a cheap apartment. We'd planned out *everything*, right down to how we were going to sneak out of the party after graduation and race to the bus station together, meeting up there and then heading out that night for Chicago.

The day of our high school graduation was a whirlwind. My father was so proud of me, and my stomach was in knots every time he patted me on the back and told me that the cap and gown looked good on me, his jaw clenched as he tried to hold back the tears in his eyes. I knew that he was proud of me; that much was obvious. For a guy with few emotions and even fewer words, this was a huge deal, his telling me that he was proud.

And that realization led, of course, to completely miserable thoughts. Thoughts like, how could I possibly leave him? How could I leave my little sister? I felt terrible, but I figured they would both be all right without me. And I was eighteen, after all, and I didn't realize that the things we do can hurt someone irrevocably. Forever.

But I was about to learn that lesson for good.

I watched Stevie accept her diploma, watched her dark brown gaze catch mine and hold it as she held the diploma aloft, her smile huge and triumphant. That day was the culmination: we had both, together, survived high school, and we thought that meant we could survive anything.

I was supposed to meet her in the afternoon at her grandparents' trailer, and we were supposed to go over the plan one more time before the party that night, go over our packing lists to make certain we hadn't missed anything.

So after the ceremony, my father took me and my sister out for celebratory ice cream, and then we drove back to the trailer park, and I was heading toward Stevie's trailer, hands deep in my jeans pockets, humming something happily as my sneakers crossed the well-worn path to Stevie's door.

But there was shouting coming from the trailer.

And the sound of an animal snarling. But Stevie's family didn't have a dog; they didn't have any animals, and certainly none that could make a sound like that.

Honestly?

It sounded like a wolf.

I didn't know what was happening, and I would never know, because Stevie came running out of the trailer, slamming the door shut behind her, tears streaming down her cheeks as she raked the back of her hand over her face, dashing the tears away. Her hair was disheveled, and—what was very odd—there was a scratch in her jeans, a six-inch-long scratch that had actually torn the fabric of the denim. Beneath the torn fabric, blood was seeping through. I stared at the cut in horror, then looked up into her eyes questioningly.

"I cut myself on the corner of the table... It's fine. You have to get out of here," said Stevie shortly, her mouth in a down-turned line. I held her gaze for a long moment as she breathed out and then gathered me close, as she pressed her nose into my hair, just as she had that first day that we met.

My skin pricked with discomfort. We always held off from embracing in public because we didn't want anyone to suspect anything, and here we were, hugging in the trailer park, in the sunshine, no less, right by the highway where anyone and everyone could see us.

I'm ashamed to say that my very first reaction was to disentangle myself from her. "Stevie," I whispered into her ear, my cheeks burning hotly.

"Don't."

She backed away a step, tears shining in her eyes. She looked as deeply pained as if I'd slapped her. But I didn't want anyone to find out about us; I didn't want anything to go wrong before we left Kankakee. Didn't she know that, once we were in Chicago, we could be ourselves? Didn't she realize that?

"Are you ashamed of me?" Stevie asked me quietly, holding my gaze.

"Baby, no," I whispered, tears springing to my eyes, too. "I just don't want anything to stop us from going," I told her, taking a step forward and curling my fingers around her elbow. "I *love* you," I whispered to her fiercely.

"Do you love me..." she whispered, licking her lips, suddenly looking afraid. Stevie *never* looked afraid, and I felt my stomach drop away from me. "Do you love me no matter what I am? Who I am?" she whispered, holding my gaze.

"Of course I do," I told her, without skipping a beat.

Stevie picked at the strands of fabric at the tear in her jeans. She tore her gaze from mine, and she looked past me, toward the train tracks and the cow fields and corn fields beyond them.

"I'll see you tonight," she told me, taking a step forward and placing a gentle, soft kiss against my cheek. Then she turned away from me, and she ran past her trailer, past the trailer park itself. She ran, alone.

I believed her. I believed that she would come. I believed with my whole heart.

And that night, I sneaked out of the party that our friend Mary was hosting for graduation. I left through the back door, and no one noticed, and I grabbed my bag from where I'd stowed it under Mary's deck. I took the bag, and I ran across the front lawn and down the street, toward the bus station. I didn't look back.

And when I got to the station, I glanced around, looking everywhere for Stevie. I thought, for some reason, that she'd already be there. She hadn't shown up to the party that night, and that had struck me as worrisome, odd.

True, it wasn't exactly strange for Stevie to skip a party. She was wild, and she did what she wanted. If she didn't want to go to the party, there was nothing on heaven or earth that could compel her to go. But uneasiness was churning in my stomach, because we'd *planned* for this. Not going to the party would look suspicious, we'd reasoned, so we would both go, and it would give us a convenient place to exit from.

But despite all that planning...Stevie hadn't shown up.

And she wasn't waiting for me at the bus station, either.

I tried to calm my racing heart, tried and failed. Already, I felt that something was wrong. Something was very wrong. But I tried to reason with myself as I sat down on the bench outside of the closed station. The bus that would come through tonight was after hours, and the station was always closed for after-hour buses. You had to have a ticket, or you weren't going to get on that bus. And I had a ticket. We both had tickets...

I tried to convince myself that Stevie had just been detained, and just for a little while. That she would arrive very, very soon, with plenty of time for the two of us to sit together and talk before the bus arrived, holding hands tightly as the thrill of our impending freedom ran through us.

But as the large clock bolted to the wall outside the station turned its hands, as it kept ticking away...

Stevie did not arrive.

Now it was getting dangerously close to the time that the bus was supposed to show up. I still, naively, believed that she was going to appear, with minutes to spare. I gripped the edge of the bench as tightly as I could, I took deep breaths, and I stared at the clock, willing it to slow down. Willing Stevie to show up, coming out of the gathering gloom of night surrounding the bus station with her bag slung over her shoulder, a happy, triumphant smile painting her features. "I'm sorry," she'd tell me, drawing me close and kissing me fiercely. "I'm sorry I'm late. It was all just a misunderstanding. But I'm here now."

And then it was time for the bus to arrive.

And Stevie was still missing.

My heart was in my throat, my blood pounding through my body as if in expectation of something terrible. My body knew already, but my mind was slow to catch up because I still believed, utterly, in Stevie. In *us*. I believed, and that meant that Stevie was going to come.

But she didn't.

The bus arrived. It pulled up, creaking and settling to a stop, in front of my bench, and a few tired, weary-looking people disembarked, taking their luggage from the doors on the side of the bus as the driver lugged them off, looking bored and unhappy.

The bus door stood open for me, but Stevie wasn't here yet. How could I get onto the bus without her?

The minutes ticked by, and I was getting so desperate, so panicked, that I could hardly breathe. "I'm sorry," I told the bus driver, fear making my words slur together, "but can you wait around for just a little while? Just a few more minutes?"

"I'm scheduled to wait for fifteen minutes," he barked at me, his handlebar mustache quivering as he swallowed another big mouthful of coffee from his enormous to-go container as he leaned against the side of the bus. "Fifteen minutes is all you get," he said with a shrug.

I slung my bag over my shoulder, took in a great gulp of air, and I bolted. I could get back to the trailer park and back here in fifteen minutes—if I ran very, *very* fast. My father and sister thought I was still at the party, so as long as they didn't see me, I might get away with this.

Stevie must have been delayed. Something was going on in her trailer earlier today. Maybe she was fighting with her grandfather again. They fought pretty frequently, and I knew that sometimes he hit her. She never hit him back, and she never looked like she was outwardly hurt from his blows, but I knew that the violence bothered her deeply, and it bothered the hell out of me.

Yeah. That must be it. They were arguing again, and she hadn't been able to get away yet. Terrible images flashed through my mind. Of her grandfather beating her up, of Stevie crying on her bed, unable to get to me.

I ran faster.

I finally reached the trailer park, my lungs aching as I tried to inhale as much air as I could, panting. It was going to be okay. If Stevie's grandfather had done something to her, he'd have to answer to me, and we would soon be away from this terrible place forever, together, just the two of us. Nothing was going to stop us.

But as I sneaked past my own trailer in the dark and angled toward hers...I began to realize that something was very, very wrong.

Stevie's grandfather's truck wasn't parked out front of the trailer, as it should be, but that wasn't the first thing that I noticed.

The first thing I noticed was the "for sale" sign picketed on the narrow strip of lawn.

It was a red sign, and it was reflective, so it reflected the lights from the streetlamps along the edge of the trailer park. I paused, staring at it, my breath coming fast as I stood there, the very fabric of the world tearing around me.

I knew before I went up and peered through the curtainless windows that there was no one inside the trailer. There were no possessions. There was nothing there.

Because Stevie and her family were gone.

I stood in the trailer park, my sides heaving as I tried to cover my mouth, tried to silence the sobs that began to wrack my body. I knew then. I knew that Stevie was truly gone. And I knew that she'd gone with her family not because they'd taken her forcibly, not because they threatened her or detained her...but because she'd wanted to go, and she'd gone of her own free will.

I can't leave my family, she'd told me often enough, repeating the words over and over again. *They need me.*

I stood alone in that trailer park, feeling my

knees buckle under me, feeling the entire weight of the universe pressing down on my narrow shoulders, bending my body until every bone within me felt like breaking, that absolute press of loneliness consuming me.

She'd chosen them over me.

It was reaching, that thought, but it seemed so much like the truth at the time, and how could this turn of events be explained away? Her family needed her, and she'd gone with them, somewhere far away. She hadn't told me she was leaving. We'd planned out *everything*, the two of us, and she'd promised me that she'd be there, that she'd go with me.

And then she'd stood me up.

I glanced at my watch on my wrist through the wash of my tears, feeling the emptiness inside eating me alive. The clock kept ticking, like it always does, and the minutes were passing, and—with them—the only opportunity I had to escape.

And then I turned on my heel and raced all the way back to the bus station, somehow managing to put one foot in front of the other as I ran, stumbling, toward my future. The bus was pulling away from the station, but I flagged the driver down. And, though he hadn't seemed the type to make allowances, the bus driver stopped for me.

I climbed up into the bus, tears streaming down my face, and I handed the man my ticket.

And I left Kankakee.

Alone.

I blink, staring at Stevie, adult Stevie, who's standing in front of me now. The memories are so real, so vibrant, that I feel as if I just relived them in the blink of an eye. The weight and pain of that night, of every night since, presses down on me. The weight of facing my father disowning me once he knew why I'd left, once he knew what I was. I faced that alone. I have faced everything, since that night, alone.

And now she's here.

She's *here*.

Stevie. The love of my life. The woman I thought I'd spend the rest of my life with...

The woman who left me alone.

I feel a great sob wracking my body, aching to be set loose, but I won't release it. Instead, I take a deep breath, my nostrils flaring as I swallow down that sob into my curdling stomach. A single tear falls from my eye, and I reach up with a shaking hand, wiping it away.

"Please," Stevie repeats, holding out a hand to me, her voice trembling. "Please come inside, Amber." And then she steps forward and whispers, "I've been looking for you for so long. Please. Give me five minutes."

Five minutes?

I stare.

She couldn't have given me five minutes to explain things seven years ago? There's no use asking her that question, because I see the pain reflected in her eyes, and though it's been seven years, yes, I still understand her, the language of her body, the very essence of all that Stevie is.

I should turn around. I should leave, and I shouldn't spare a single glance backward.

Seven years ago, Stevie didn't have the decency to tell me that she wasn't coming with me. Seven years ago, we had a connection that I thought meant we were soulmates.

I loved her with every atom in my body, with every last part of my soul.

And she, obviously, had not felt the same way.

How else could she have left me standing there alone? How else could she disappear without a single explanation?

How else, other than the fact that she didn't love me, after all?

"Five. Minutes," Stevie breathes, holding my gaze, her deep brown eyes seeing to the very depths of me. Or, at least, that's what it feels like.

Five minutes.

I don't know why I do it. I shouldn't. I know I shouldn't. But, somehow, I feel myself nodding, holding tightly onto my purse strap as if it's a lifeline, as if I'm about to fall away into an abyss if I let go.

Five minutes. I can survive five minutes. Can't I? Because, in five minutes, I can learn so much. After all this time, I still need to know. I need to understand.

Why did she leave me that night?

I know that this is opening me up to enormous heartache. But the wounds of the past never healed. I have to know, because wondering all of these years has nearly driven me crazy. I *need to know*.

So Stevie turns, gestures down the concrete staircase. She wants me to go first, maybe just to make sure that I'm not going to turn and leave.

But I wasn't the one who left.

I swallow down the bile and sobs rising in my throat, and I walk down the concrete steps, my heels clicking on the cement. And Stevie follows. I inhale the scent of her, the scent of her that hasn't changed, even after all these years. She still carries that perfume of wildness with her, of an overgrown wood and crisp, sharp air, like you're walking in the forest, leaves falling all around you. It's an October scent.

I'm so distracted by my thoughts and feelings that I barely notice that Jessica, the woman who'd been screwing in the new sign, appears from somewhere behind us, following at a distance, her eyes pointed down to the ground discreetly.

It takes a long moment for my eyes to adjust to the interior of the club. I stand still, waiting for Stevie to move past me. But she doesn't. Instead, she stands next to me, reaches up, and she places her hand against the small of my back, her palm flat against me, gentle and soft...tentative.

I turn to look up at her, my heart racing.

She used to do this; she used to do this all the time, and I'm ashamed to think of all of the daydreams I've had where she comes back to me and does exactly this. In those dreams, I'm standing on the shore of the river, at the bend, next to the shack that stands there no longer... I'm standing, and I'm staring out at the swirling, muddy waters, and then I feel a light pressure at the small of my back. I look up, and Stevie is standing next to me. She isn't much taller than me—just an inch, really—but it was just tall enough that, whenever I kissed her, I lifted my chin and drank her in deeply.

In the dreams, I would turn and she would wrap her arms tightly around me, and we would kiss each other hard, passionately. We meant that kiss with every fiber of our beings.

But it was just a dream. And when I woke up, I was still alone.

Here and now, I feel the pressure of Stevie's fingertips at the small of my back, the lightness of her palm pressing against me, and I take a step forward. I can't bear it, can't bear that reassuring weight, the weight that has not been there for seven years. That does not deserve to be there now.

"Five minutes," I tell her, my jaw clenched. "That's all I'm giving you. And I shouldn't even give you that much," I whisper.

She holds my gaze in the darkness of the club, and her eyes are sad, aching, but there are no tears on her cheeks. She nods once, twice, resolute, gesturing behind me.

"My office is this way," she says, voice low and soft. Gruff.

I glance around me at the inside of the club. I've never been in here, but I'm able to tell just from looking around that the inside of it has changed quite a bit in recent weeks. There's sawdust on the floor, and there are old bar cabinets ripped out, dismantled and piled neatly in the corner, waiting to be laid to rest in a Dumpster. There are new cabinets, ones that look very modern, chrome and sleek, being installed by several people who are very carefully avoiding glancing in our direction. I can only assume that my near-shouting was audible through the open door.

A power saw roars to life in the background, and I nod, suddenly feeling self-conscious as I make a beeline for the only hallway leading out of the main area of the club.

Stevie moves with me, and we're walking along the darkened corridor together. I close my eyes, my heart aching inside of me. Was this a mistake? Giving her five minutes? Yeah...this was probably a mistake.

We're not even speaking, and I can feel the weight and the pain of seven years crushing me.

As we near the end of the hallway, walking together, the sound of her footfalls so familiar, Stevie opens a door ahead of us, and we step through.

She flicks on the light, shutting the door behind us.

And we're alone.

I turn around and stare at her, and she stares at me. Her arms are folded in front of her, and the pain on her face is evident in the dim lamplight, but neither of us speaks for a very long moment.

"You look good, Amber," she finally says, quietly, haltingly. "You look really good," she whispers to me.

I stare at her, the pain of the years pressing down on me so heavily that I feel like I can't breathe. I want to ask her a million things; I want to cry and scream. But somehow I find in myself the last shred of strength I possess. And I ask her the one question that matters, the question I sobbed into my pillow for years, the question that has haunted me every single day. "Why?" I whisper to her. That single word encapsulates seven long years of pain, a single syllable to symbolize all of my darkness and sadness.

One word. And it's enough.

She lifts her chin, holding my gaze with her beautiful, dark brown eyes, those eyes that have haunted my dreams every night.

"I'm sorry," she whispers then. She says exactly what I've ached to hear for far too long. She gives me an apology. And with those words, I can feel the weight of her sorrow, can feel the weight of time and promises made and promises broken.

"I'm...I'm *sorry*," she repeats, and she reaches up and presses her hand flat over her heart, pressing down on her skin, as if she can press away the ache, the hurt.

And that's when a single tear leaks out of her right eye, tracing down her cheek and falling away from her face. She holds my gaze, but there is so much hurt, so much pain in her eyes that it takes my breath away.

She takes my breath away.

No. No. I'm not supposed to think that, feel that. One apology doesn't fix things, doesn't erase the pain. It doesn't begin to amend or atone for the debilitating ache that unfurls in your heart when you believe, utterly, that your life is going to go one way, and then it doesn't. It goes in the complete opposite direction.

But Stevie is standing in front of me. She's pressing a hand against her heart because the ache inside of her is so great. The pain that washes over her beautiful face is deep, vulnerable, raw.

So my body moves on instinct now. I can't help it, I can't help any of it, as I take a single, tentative step forward, and I reach up...

And with the pad of my thumb, I wipe away the streak of her tear across her cheek.

She closes her eyes. Her nostrils flare as she breathes out, as she sighs, as she presses the side of her face against my palm. She closes her eyes, her black lashes fluttering against her cheeks, just as they did when I first met her, when I first saw the girl who would become the woman I would love with my whole heart. She moves her warm cheek against my palm, and something inside of me breaks. Melts. Dissolves.

"I'm sorry," Stevie repeats, whispering the words, breathing out with a sigh.

"Why?" I repeat, as she opens her eyes, as we stare at one another. She searches my face, worry making her brow furrow. She still presses her cheek against my palm, and I stay there, standing, touching her gently.

"I had to," she tells me then gruffly, and she takes a step backward, and we are no longer touching. She leans back against the wall, shaking her head, lifting her eyes to the heavens as she takes a deep breath, sniffs. "I had to," she repeats, looking at me again, her eyes blazing with an inner fire I don't quite understand.

"That's...it?" I ask, when she says nothing else for a long moment. "Just...you *had* to? Why didn't you tell me that you weren't able to go? Why did you just stand me up? Why did you just...disappear?" I ask her, the aching scars inside of my heart making it difficult for me to force out the words.

We stare at one another for a long moment. There's only a small space separating us; Stevie's office isn't all that big. There's one step, really, between our bodies. One step forward. If I lifted my hand right now, I could reach up and touch her. And I almost do, my fingers twitching as I curl them into fists, curling them so that they don't betray me.

"I can't tell you," is Stevie's maddening reply.

"*What?*" My voice is loud, angry, but I can't help it. I'm yelling now, tears streaming down my cheeks. "How could you even say that? How could *that* be your answer, after all of these years? You *disappeared*. You...you *evaporated* right out of my life when I...when I needed you most..." My chest is heaving with sobs that I'm trying to quell, but I can't.

One great, wracking sob escapes me, and then the tears are all that I can see.

I draw in a deep breath, wiping away the tears and sniffling. "I loved you so much," I whisper to her, swallowing the lump in my throat.

I hate this. I hate how vulnerable, how pathetic I'm acting in front of her, the woman who left me. But this is me. This is the truth. My love for her was the truest thing I knew once, the most absolute truth. I loved her with my body, heart and soul, and she disappeared from my life forever. For no reason. For *no reason.*

Well, there must have been a reason. But as we stare at one another, emotions heavy between us, I can see the war waging over Stevie's face. She wants to tell me. But she can't. Why in the world would she not be able to tell me this?

I swallow another sob, bury my face in my hands. My heart aches so much that I can hardly breathe.

Finally, Stevie clears her throat. I glance up at her through my tears, see the soft gentleness on her face that she always used to show me, and my insides are unraveling again. It would be so much easier if we were still yelling. Her kindness, her sympathy, is something I don't know how to handle, or endure.

"I'm sorry, Amber," Stevie whispers then, her voice shaking. But she keeps her words level, soft, and she lifts her chin, her dark brown eyes flashing in the dim light of the room. "You wouldn't believe me, even if I told you the truth of what happened that night," she says gently. "I did everything in my power to...to..." She rakes her hand through her ponytail, shaking her head. She's obviously agitated as she pushes off from the desk, as she takes a single step toward me. "To keep you safe," she breathes.

We're together, in that moment, almost touching. She wants to kiss me. I think she wants to kiss me. I don't know. I don't know anything.

But my body betrays me. My heart betrays me, betrays all the nights of pain, all the nights I sobbed myself to sleep and dreamed about a life I would never, could never have.

I lift my chin; I eradicate the space between us. I lean forward.

And I kiss her.

Seven years is a long time. A long, long time, eighty-four months full of regret, sadness and heartache... And it feels as if more than seven years have come and gone. It feels like I've lived a lifetime in Stevie's absence.

But, at the same time, it also feels like I last saw Stevie only a moment ago, just yesterday, or this morning. Like she stepped out of a room and then came back—changed a little, sure, but back all the same. Back in my arms. Kissing me again.

I remember what it was like to kiss Stevie. I remember how she tasted, what her lips and tongue felt like against my own. I remember how she would smile against me, how she would tilt her head to the side, just a little, so that she could press closer, closer...so that we could merge.

Now, she tilts her head, just a little. She tastes of peppermint gum, the rush of coolness against my mouth a shocking sensation as it mingles with the warmth of her skin. I drink her in, the coolness of the mint, the heat of all that she is, and as I kiss her, as I reach up and wrap my arms around her shoulders, I find that I'm crying again, silent tears leaking out of the corners of my eyes as I do the one thing that I'd wished for, all those seven years.

I kiss Stevie. And Stevie kisses me back.

Slowly she reaches up, wrapping her long fingers around my curves until her hands meet at the small of my back. She presses her palms there, her warm, comforting palms that radiate heat through the cloth of my shirt, into my skin.

All of the deep pain that I have felt for seven years is pulsing through me, matching the rhythm of my blood, but it's battling the fact that I'm standing here, right now, and I'm kissing her. I'm kissing the woman that I couldn't push out of my thoughts, the woman who haunted me every day, every night. Every moment since she left. I never heard from her; she never tried to come for me, to find me. She left me alone.

Still, I have never been able to stop thinking about her. I've never been able to stop wanting her.

And she's here, now. And she's kissing me back.

She wants me, too.

And it is because of this, and because of all of my wants, all of my dreams, all of my deepest desires, rising like a tidal wave inside of my body, that I am powerless to hold back, to pull away, to insist upon an explanation, to make her explain.

I press the front of my body against hers as she leans forward to meet me. She draws me to her, her hands tighter now against the small of my back. And as I tilt my head up, as I open my eyes take in her own eyes—close, so close to mine—I see the furrow in her brow. She's worried, conflicted, just as much as I am.

No.

For this moment, just this moment...I don't want to think about *anything*.

There's no past, no future.

All we have is here, now.

I take a step back from her, panting. I am so vulnerable, so open to new, fresh wounds. If she rejects me, if she rejects me again... I swallow down my misgivings. It takes the most courage I have ever had to reach up with shaking fingers and undo the top button of my blouse.

I watch her gaze travel down from my eyes to that opened button, to the curve of my clavicle, visible in the V of my shirt. I see her eyes drift over my skin, watch them ignite with sparks of desire.

And that response from her is all that it takes for my shaking hands to stop shaking, for my fingers to progress to the second button, and the third. By the fourth, I'm undoing each button faster, boldly, my breath coming quicker. And by the time that the entire front of my blouse is open, Stevie is pressing against me again, pressing me back against the wall as she covers my mouth with her own, as her hot palms and fingers graze the skin of my stomach, as she pushes the blouse down over my shoulders. The shirt's sleeves pool around my wrists, and the light fabric drifts down to rest at my waist as I shiver against her, the sensuality of the cloth drifting over my skin, of the heat of her hands, enough to light a fire that roars through me.

For seven years, I have dreamed of a moment like this. I have had dreams, memories, really, of how Stevie made me feel, how I felt when we were together. How she tasted, the sensation of her skin beneath my fingertips. The memory of her fingertips touching me. I have daydreamed about it so often that sometimes I wondered whether I was only half-living, whether I lived in my dreams rather than in my day-to-day life... Because my day-to-day life is miserable, fraught with confusion, pain, and regret.

But here, now, I know I'm not dreaming, and it seems almost impossible as I reach forward, as I curl my fingers under the edge of Stevie's tank top. My fingertips rest against the searing heat of her skin... *Searing*. Why is she so *hot*? She's almost feverish...

I chalk it up to the fact that we both want each other. That we both *need* each other. That this is so many years overdue.

I inch up the fabric of Stevie's tank top so that I can grip her hips with my hands—just as she reaches up, passing the pad of her thumb over the skin of my breast, above the lace edge of my bra. It's tantalizing: just a sweet, soft touch, but there's such fire in her skin, in her fingertips, as she tugs the cup of the bra down, tugs it down with purpose. My breast comes free, and she presses the fabric of the bra beneath my breast. She leans down now, wasting no time, and she draws my nipple into her mouth in one smooth motion.

Little explosions of light dance behind my eyes as I gasp out loud, as I rear back my head, arching my body against her, desperate for more connection, for more feeling as Stevie wraps her arm around my waist, drawing me ever closer to her as she flicks my nipple with her tongue, grazing her teeth over the edge of it. She looks up at me, her dark brown eyes glittering with desire, and then she bites down harder.

Harder, harder...just hard enough that it's an exquisite, pleasurable bloom of softest pain, but nothing more than that. It's like she knows exactly what I want, somehow—but then...she does, doesn't she? There were so many times in the past that she made my body sing, playing it like an instrument that she knew, instinctively, almost better than her own body. She knows me, yes, she knows exactly what I like, and that's *exactly* what's she's doing to me right now.

It's like no time has passed at all as I gasp against her, as she reaches for the button and zipper on my jeans and I close my eyes.

We exist outside of time, no past or future, as her fingers undo that single button, brushing against the skin of my stomach. She holds my gaze as she slowly unzips the zipper, her fingers curling around the waistband of my jeans, curling strongly. She tugs the jeans down around my hips, then around my thighs, but she doesn't pull them off of me completely.

And somehow that makes everything hotter: her fingers drift up and over my sex, my panties already completely soaked through.

It's the eye contact, I think, panting as she holds my gaze, holds my gaze and rubs her thumb over my clit through the fabric of the panties. It's how completely sure she is, going through each motion like a well-rehearsed dance, devoid of nonsense or uncertainty, totally and completely sure as she teases me, dipping her head again, tasting my breast, tugging down the bra cup over my left breast and tasting that one, too, trailing wet kisses between them. My breasts strain up over the bunched up fabric of the bra, and I gasp a little as she reaches up, pinching the right one as she sucks and licks and bites the left.

My center is aching, and the jeans are bunched up right at the top of my thighs, so when she steps forward, when she presses her thigh between my legs, it's delicious, that sensation, that pressure. I moan a little, trying to be quiet (how thin are these walls? The power-sawing stopped a little while ago).

Stevie moves in gracefully, standing tall and kissing me hard. The pressure of her leg at my center is bold, but it's not enough, and she knows this, so she starts to rhythmically move against me, her strength the only thing holding me up now as my knees almost give out from the pleasure roaring through me as she moves against me, as I thrust my hips against her, desperate and wanting.

She knows this, and she dips her head low again, pressing a kiss to my peaked right nipple, my hard nipple that she takes in her mouth again, licking gently now, as if to tease me. I sigh, biting my lip, trying to keep the moan inside of me as Stevie traces her fingers down the front of my stomach, down and under the waistband of my panties. Her fingers are curling up as her palm presses against my skin, and then she finds out exactly how wet I am.

She smiles against my breast, and I can feel that smile, and then she's lifting her head, kissing me deeply, thrusting her tongue into my mouth as I gasp out. She curves her fingers into me as she kisses me.

God, it's so good, but there are no words for this moment, so my body does all of the talking. I'm thrusting my hips against her thigh, against her hand, and I'm riding her as much as I'm able, my knees weak, waves of pleasure and want already rocketing through me. Seven years have come and gone, and it's been awhile since my last one-night stand, so maybe I'm a little rusty... Maybe my leg muscles just aren't strong enough for this sort of thing. But it doesn't matter, because Stevie knows, of course she knows, and her other arm curls around my waist again, but this time with enough firmness, with enough strength, to hold me up.

I press the flat of my left foot against the floor as hard as I can, and then I wrap my right leg around her waist, spreading my legs further for her, wider, but not wide enough. That "not enough" feeling is delicious as my legs strain against the pooled fabric of the jeans, as Stevie moves in, slipping a third finger inside of me now as she straightens a little, holding my gaze again with those wildly beautiful brown eyes.

They flash with flecks of gold as she holds me tightly, as her eyes narrow with desire, as she she pumps her fingers into me harder, faster. I want to look away—God, this is too vulnerable, locking eyes with someone I once loved so much...who left me so long ago, scarring me irrevocably. To be this open to her again, this deeply exposed, makes my heart ache.

But I know, know as she touches me, as she reaches deep inside of me and finds the perfect pleasure that has eluded me all of these years (no one could ever compare to Stevie), that I never really stopped loving her. God, I wanted to. I wanted to let her go, the person who had hurt me the most in my life.

But I never could.

I'm filled with that love, rising inside of me, as she holds my gaze, as I see into the very deepest parts of her. Her mouth opens slightly, and her wet lips open, and her breathing begins to come harder.

She wants me to come. That desire, that want, that need inside of her rockets through me, and I find pleasure rising in me so quickly, so triumphantly, that I have to throw my head back. I'm seeing stars.

The orgasm crests as quickly as a tidal wave,

rushing through me. Every atom I possess feels the power and the pleasure of it as my body moves against Stevie, as I wrap my arms around her, moaning out, feeling somehow, in that moment, that the two of us aren't *two* anymore... We're moving together. As one.

Stevie keeps massaging her thumb against my clit, keeps slowly moving her fingers in and out of me, drawing out the orgasm, drawing it out to the very last note my body can feel before it's just too much. Then, and only then, does she withdraw her fingers as I tremble against her. She traces a wet line, gliding her fingertips over my skin, until she's curling her hand around my hip again, then wrapping both of her arms around me, drawing me as close as I'm holding her. The two of us are wrapped up in one another now, my leg still hooked around her middle.

We're merged, Stevie and me.

As much as the orgasm was good, bone-deep incredible, I find myself wanting her again within a few heartbeats. Maybe it's the scent of her, as I bury my nose in her hair, the wildness that I can still smell on her skin, the deep, woody scent of the forest. She smells just like she used to, and that is the most comforting scent in the world to me. But it's also the one that makes me want the most.

I draw my leg down, and then I'm standing on my own two feet again as Stevie eases out from between my legs, straightening and shifting her weight to back in her heels. Her eyes are glinting with happiness as she smiles down at me, but then I'm tugging at the waistband of her tank top, drawing it up over her muscled stomach.

My God, when did she start working out? I mean, it was obvious when I saw her biceps that she was more muscled than she used to be, but as I pull up her tank top, I stare at the chiseled six-pack that the Stevie I knew *never* had...

And I stop.

"What..." I whisper, taking in her shape, her skin.

There's a long, angry, puckered white scar that traces down from the top left side of her abs, all the way down and disappearing beneath the band of her pants.

I don't know why, but in that moment I remember the last time I saw Stevie. I remember the blood beneath her jeans, the cut in the denim...

Did this scar happen that day?

"Stevie, what is this?" I whisper, looking up at her. Her eyes have lost the glittering sparks of desire: they're dark now, dark with pain as she reaches up, rolling down her tank top again to cover her stomach.

She turns away from me, and I suddenly feel cold.

I pull my pants up over my bottom again, doing up the button and zipping the zipper with shaking hands. I suddenly feel very self-conscious as I pull up the cups of my bra, drawing the fabric of my shirt down, folding my arms in front of me.

"Stevie, what *happened* to you?" I whisper, my voice shaking. "It looks like you were ripped in *half*."

Because it does. I've seen scars before. I have a pretty rotten one from a bike-riding accident when I was twelve, when I ripped my calf open going over a pretty rocky path near the trailer park on an old bike that really couldn't handle it. I needed twenty-five stitches that day, and the skin is as white as snow where the wound healed.

But this scar... This scar looks like the result of an enormous, jagged cut. Like Stevie was ripped open by...*something*, and then her skin tried to heal as best as it could. But you can't ever perfectly heal something so torn apart.

For a long moment, I feel the chasm yawning between us again, the chasm of silence that drove Stevie to disappear from my life. She didn't tell me what was wrong then, but something *must* have been wrong for her to vanish, for her to betray my trust, betray our love, to stand me up when I'd really believed that she was going to run away with me...

That's what had been so hard, all these years. I had believed, utterly, that she was going to show up that night.

And then she just...didn't.

We hadn't argued. We'd both been certain about our plans, and our feelings for each other.

It didn't add up. It didn't make any sense.

"Please, Stevie," I whisper, wrapping my arms around myself tightly. I was so vulnerable to her a moment ago, and it takes every last remnant of my strength to be vulnerable to her again. But I have to be, in this moment. I ask her, "Please, Stevie... Tell me what happened to you."

Stevie turns then, and the pain in her eyes is so deep, so anguished that it shocks me to my core. There is so much suffering in her face as she turns toward me, as her arms drop open at her sides. Her ponytail is a little tousled from when I reached up and held her head, cradling it against my heart as she tasted me... That tiny incongruity, with the pain on her face, hits me right in the heart.

"I can never tell you," Stevie whispers to me.

Her hands curl into fists, and then she's lifting her chin, the pain so deep in her eyes that she looks, in this moment, like she's dying. "I can't," Stevie whispers, "because if you knew..." She trails off, then turns away, raking a hand through her hair and moaning out in frustration. "I have done *everything*," she whispers, sobbing the word out as she turns back to me. "*Everything*," she whispers again, her hands hanging limply at her sides, "to keep you safe."

And then Stevie moves, crouching down in one, smooth motion. She crouches down, and then she's kneeling in front of me.

And she very slowly, very carefully, wraps her arms around my legs, pressing her face to my stomach as hot tears begin to spill down her cheeks.

"Please, forgive me," she begs me softly. "Everything I've done, I've done it for you."

Stevie kneels in front of me, has gathered me tightly in her arms. This moment of raw weakness, of openness, is so unexpected. But this is how she used to be, I remember. Before she disappeared. This is how much she trusted me before, laying down her deepest secrets and darkest nightmares. It's how we both were, and how we drew so close together, entwined in one another's hearts.

Everything I've done, I've done it for you.

I reach out, and I softly, gently, rest my fingers upon her hair. There's so much love rising in my heart; all I am is love. God, I loved her once. I never stopped loving her.

But I have been through so much, too. So much pain, so much grief, so much loss since she walked out of my life without an explanation. I am deeply wounded, deeply scarred, and I need answers.

"What happened that night, Stevie?" I whisper to her as she breathes me in, as she presses her mouth, her nose to my stomach, as she closes her eyes tightly.

And then she sags against me, the firmness of her muscles receding. She leans against me, her entire weight, but I can hold her up. I've held her up before. We've both held each other up. We've both been there for each other in every way, in every thing.

Stevie rises then, wiping away her own tears, breathing out in resolve. She holds my gaze as she wraps her hands gently around my shoulders, holding tightly to me.

"Something happened," she whispers, her eyes wide, hurting. I hold her gaze, the pain punching me in the gut, but I do my best to stay strong for her. "Something really bad happened, Amber," she whispers so softly that I have to strain to hear her.

I listen.

And Stevie takes a deep breath, and she lets the air out slowly, her nostrils flaring. "My grandfather attacked me the day of graduation," she whispers, her right hand uncurling from my shoulder. She presses the flat of her palm against her stomach. "He gave me this," she says now, her jaw clenched, the words coming out in a growl.

"*What?*" I whisper. I knew Stevie's grandparents weren't exactly good people, but how could her grandfather have possibly given her that scar? What did he *use*? A knife? A piece of broken glass?

How could he hurt his granddaughter so terribly? *Why* would he do something so reprehensible? So gut-wrenchingly, nauseatingly awful?

Stevie's jaw is clenched so tightly that her veins are throbbing in her forehead. She tries to relax again as she swallows, as she takes a step back from me, shaking her head. "I've done everything so that you would never find out," she whispers to me, pleading. "I don't want you to know what happened," she says, her arms falling slack at her sides, "because if you know, you'll never want to see me again. I've tried, so hard, to find you," she tells me quickly now, taking a step forward. "I'm so sorry for that night, for my disappearing... Couldn't we try again? Couldn't you give me another chance...without...knowing?"

"Your grandfather hurt you," I say her in a low whisper, reaching out and touching her arm gently. "What could *you* have done to make me never want to see you again? You've already hurt me, Stevie," I whisper to her.

"No. This is so much worse," she tells me softly, looking away.

What could she be keeping a secret from me? I stand there, completely uncertain, as she rakes her hand over her hair in frustration again. She groans a little, rocking back on her heels, then sitting on her desk and gripping the edge of it until her knuckles turn white.

"How can I bear losing you again?" she asks me, pinning me down with her mournful brown gaze.

Stunned by her words, I stand still and gaze deeply into her eyes, searching, aching. "I...I thought I'd never see you again," I murmur, trying to find the right words, words that aren't full of resentment or blame. I do my best. "You disappeared. For seven *years*, Stevie," I whisper, as her eyes darken with pain, "you were a ghost. I just...I thought I'd never see you again," I repeat, "so I never had the luxury of believing I could find you. That there was even a *possibility* that I could lose you *again*. I'd already lost you, and I never knew why." I hold my hands out to her now, my heart breaking. "I loved you so much, and you left. You can't make up for that," I tell her, lifting my chin, "but you can tell me the truth so that I can—finally—understand. I *deserve* to know, Stevie. Why did you leave that night? What *happened* to you?"

Stevie's eyes glitter in the half-light of the room as she holds my gaze. Then she closes her eyes, grips the edge of the desk tightly. "My grandfather's teeth made that scar, Amber," she whispers quietly. "Because my grandfather was a werewolf."

Of all of the things in the world that I might have been expecting to hear, this wasn't even in the same universe. And I am so deeply hurt by her words, hurt that she would twist my pain like a knife, turn it into such a pathetic joke. I gasp out, holding my hand against my stomach as my eyes fill with tears, as I stagger backward, trying to figure out the quickest way I can exit this room, this club.

But Stevie opens her eyes again, their color dull with pain. "Let me show you," she whispers, her voice heavy.

And then everything I know, everything I *think* I know, is revised, reversed.

Because Stevie pushes off from the desk, and then she's bending forward in one graceful swoop and...

I'm not really certain what happens next. It's hard to describe. It's like her spine lengthens, and her nose grows a little longer. That's impossible... And it's impossible that, instead of Stevie, there is something *else* standing in front of me right now.

The room is dimly lit, it's true, but soft lighting can't explain away the fact that there is now a wolf standing, panting, in front of me.

The wolf is tall, her back even with my hips, which is really big to me, especially in this enclosed space. She has long fur, gray mixed with white, massive paws, a bushy tail and elegantly peaked ears.

But what guts me to my core is her eyes.

The deep, dark warmth of those deep, dark brown eyes. The eyes that I know, eyes that have haunted my dreams for seven years.

Is this real? Am I hallucinating?

The wolf stands perfectly still, only occasionally blinking, her sides rising and falling as she breathes steadily. And that's when I find the courage to take a step forward, to sink down to my heels in a crouch.

I'm kneeling in front of the impossible wolf. I don't know where I'm finding this bravery from, but I must have a little left in me, because I'm lifting up my hand, and I'm brushing my fingers over the wolf's ruff.

She closes her eyes, sighing out.

And then I bring my hand forward, and I press my palm against the side of the wolf's face, cradling her head in my hand.

And the wolf presses her head gently against me, breathing out, eyes closed. Vulnerable, utterly.

God.

Yes.

This is Stevie.

Her underfur is soft against my fingers, but her wiry hair is a little coarse. I can *feel* that, can feel the realness of this moment, of her, against my palm. I reach up with my other hand, and I trace the pad of my thumb over the slope of her skull, down her narrow muzzle, and to the tip of her cold, wet nose.

This is *real*.

This is *Stevie*.

I'm weeping, then, as I wrap my arms around the wolf's neck, as I bury my face in her fur. I'm weeping hard, tears streaming down my face, as I realize the magnitude of what has happened, of what happened to Stevie that night, so long ago.

And she was alone. She dealt with it all alone.

Suddenly my arms are no longer wrapped around fur and muscle but around a woman's body I know so well. Stevie. She transformed in my arms, and now her arms are wrapped tightly around me, too, and tears streak down her face as we sit together, the two of us, on her office floor.

"My grandfather was bitten when he was a boy," she's saying now, the words stuttering out of her mouth as she finally allows herself to tell the story. "He lived in rural Pennsylvania, and there was a werewolf who bit him. He hid it from my grandmother until their wedding night, and somehow, my grandmother was able to stick by his side. He was so afraid that his kids would turn out to be werewolves, but it never happened. Sometimes he couldn't control his temper, and when he lost control of his temper, he couldn't control his wolf...

"So the day we were supposed to leave, I was packing—and he found me. Caught me. He was so mad, he couldn't stop his transformation, so he became a wolf, and he tore into me before my grandmother could calm him down," whispers Stevie, holding me at arm's length as she lifts up the hem of her tank top, showing me the scar again.

I reach out and gently, oh, so gently, trace a single finger down the line of that angry scar. Stevie shivers against me but doesn't shy away, and I reach up then to cup her face, to draw her close to me again.

"When you first transform...you can't control it," whispers Stevie then, letting her forehead fall to my shoulder. Her words are halting, broken. "So I would be me one moment, and then part wolf, and then all wolf... And I was savage, because I hadn't learned to tame the wolf yet. Amber, I couldn't let you see me that way. My grandfather convinced me that if you saw me that way, you would never love me. That you would *hate* me."

She lifts her gaze again; its intensity holds me in place. "He told me that I was a monster, just like him, and that I would kill you if you came near me. I wanted to protect you... I loved you," she whispers brokenly, speaking the words like a prayer. "I *love* you," she revises, releasing the words between us.

My entire worldview has been altered—and so quickly. I don't know what to think anymore; it seems that the universe that I thought I knew, thought I understood...isn't real at all. Or, rather, it's only a half-truth, because werewolves *exist*. What else might exist?

What else don't I know?

I shake my head. Now isn't the time for existential wonderings.

Because above everything else, even above the fact that Stevie just transformed into a *wolf*...

I blink slowly, shaking my head again, drawing the woman in my arms closer.

My world is irrevocably changed. But Stevie is here. I would have thought it impossible, a few hours ago, that my greatest wish could ever come true. I thought I'd live out the rest of my life miserable and alone, always wondering why.

But Stevie is back, *found*. My soulmate, found. The woman I love with my whole heart loves me still.

And maybe she's changed; maybe she's different now... Well, let's be honest: she's a werewolf, and that's going to take some getting used to.

But we're together.

And she loves me.

"I love you," I tell her then, and I have to repeat it, because my words come out so choked, it's hard to tell what I said. "I *love* you," I say again, the words strong and unbroken this time as I grip her tightly. "I thought... I thought you left me because you didn't want to be with me. I thought... God, I thought so many terrible things," I tell her, shaking my head.

"I have hurt *so much* for the past seven years," I whisper, "and I understand now," I say, searching her eyes. "I understand why you left. But I wish you hadn't. It didn't matter to me, Stevie. It *doesn't* matter to me. All I wanted was you. I would have found a way to make it all right. I would have found a way," I whisper vehemently.

Stevie grips my hands now, shaking her head. "We can't... We can't go back in time, Amber," she says then, lifting her chin. "Though I've wished, a million times, that I could."

"Me, too," I whisper.

"We can't go back in time," she repeats, "but we can go forward. We can go forward together. If you...if you..." Her voice breaks.

"I love you," I tell her again, wrapping my arms around her, "and I've never stopped loving you, and I will never stop loving you. No matter what you are, who you are..."

She's laughing against me through her tears, shaking her head. "I'm a *werewolf*, Amber, and that doesn't make you the tiniest bit alarmed?"

"I figure it's not like the movies or books," I answer tentatively, "but I realize I have a lot to learn. It doesn't matter, though. Not really. Because you're *Stevie*. And I've loved Stevie my whole life," I tell her. It's the truth, the deepest truth I know.

Stevie rises then, helping me up, her arms wrapped around my waist as she lifts me. We hold onto each other, our combined strength holding one another up.

"I'm sorry it took me so long to find you," Stevie whispers. "But I hope I'll have the rest of my life to make up for that...to make up for everything."

All of the years of sadness, of despair, of pain, begin to fall away from me as I gaze into her soft, love-filled brown eyes.

"You don't have to make up for anything."

Stevie sacrificed her own happiness to keep me safe, and all of the stories I'd invented in my head about why she didn't show up that night were only that: stories. "Let's just... Let's just start over," I tell her with a deep sigh.

Stevie's full lips curl up at the corners as she squeezes me gently. "All right, then. How's this? Once upon a time, there was a werewolf who loved a human woman very, very much."

"Mm. I like the sound of that." I stand up on my tiptoes and kiss her.

Around us, the new club Wolf Queen prepares for opening night.

And I hold my own wolf queen tightly.

I'm never letting her go again.

The End

Made in the USA
Middletown, DE
29 April 2016